Chicken Mission

Danger in the Deep Dark Woods

Jennifer Gray lives in London and Scotland with her husband, four children and friendly but enigmatic cat, Henry. Her other work includes the Atticus Claw series and the Guinea Pigs Online books, co-written with Amanda Swift. The first book in the Atticus series, *Atticus Claw Breaks the Law*, was shortlisted for the Waterstone's Children's Book Prize and won the 2014 Red House Children's Book Award – Younger Readers category.

BY THE SAME AUTHOR

Atticus Claw Breaks the Law

Atticus Claw Settles a Score

Atticus Claw Lends a Paw

Atticus Claw Goes Ashore

Chicken Mission

Danger in the Deep Dark Woods

JENNIFER GRAY

FABER & FABER

First published in 2014
by Faber & Faber Limited
Bloomsbury House, 74–77 Great Russell Street,
London WC1B 3DA

Printed in the UK by CPI Group (UK) Ltd, Croydon, CR0 4YY

A CIP record for this book
is available from the British Library

ISBN 978–0–571–29827–3

2 4 6 8 10 9 7 5 3 1

To Bruce and Roger

With special thanks to Sarah and family,
and the chickens of Thatched House

Prologue

High in the mountains of Tibet, far away from the hustle and bustle of humans, lies an abandoned monastery. It is populated by birds; poultry, to be precise. Poultry have many enemies and it is here, to the International School of Kung Fu for Poultry, that they flock from around the world to learn the art of battle.

On this particular day in the depths of a biting winter, a magnificent black cockerel with shiny green tail feathers and a scarlet comb sat in a mahogany wing chair beside a roaring log fire, reading from a folder. Opposite him an ancient emu with a black silk band tied around its head stood on one leg. Its eyes were closed. Its breath whistled in and out of its beak.

The cockerel, whose name was Professor Emeritus Rooster, looked up from the folder. 'Are you sure you can do it?' he asked the emu. 'I mean three young chickens with no previous martial arts experience don't make the most obvious crack team of warriors.'

Another much younger emu – this time with a red band wrapped around its head – poured some green tea into a china cup that stood on a table beside the professor. 'Do not disturb the great Shigong Egg,' he whispered. 'The Ouj-jay leg-neck knot requires great concentration. Only he can achieve it without falling over.'

Professor Rooster put down the folder. He sipped his tea and glanced out of the window. The monastery was perched on a rock. Outside in the snow-covered yard, rows of birds in silk pyjamas were being put through judo moves by two black-belted swans. There was nowhere better than the International School of Kung Fu for Poultry for three young chickens to learn combat. And no one better than Shigong Egg, the Highest Bird of Martial Arts, to teach them.

Even so, it was a risk.

Shigong Egg's breathing became heavier. Slowly the ancient bird opened one wing, then the other.

Then he gradually lifted the raised leg and twisted it around his neck until his foot met his knee joint. He tied the leg in an elegant knot around his long scrawny neck. The emu's eyes opened. 'Ah,' he said, 'Professor Rooster. Forgive me. That is the most difficult part of the posture. What were you saying?'

'I . . . er . . .' Professor Rooster gave a little cough. He didn't want to be the one who disturbed the great Shigong Egg's concentration. If he fell over like that, he could strangle himself. 'Wouldn't you rather sit down?' he suggested.

Shigong Egg shook his head slowly. 'It is kind of you, Professor. But for Shigong Egg, the Ou-jay leg-neck knot is the most comfortable position for contemplation. Please continue.'

Professor Rooster decided to come straight to the point. 'Shouldn't I just hire a professional poultry protector?' he said. 'I mean what's the use of three kid chickens against one of the world's most devious villains?'

'Young minds are more ingenious than old.' Shigong Egg bent forward towards the floor. 'Have confidence, Professor. The young chickens I have selected for your mission each have a special skill. One has courage. One has intelligence. The other has perseverance. Together they will make the greatest elite chicken combat force the world has ever known.'

Professor Rooster glanced at the folder. It contained the profiles of the three chickens Shigong Egg had chosen for the mission. 'But none of them knows anything about martial arts,' he said doubtfully. 'And only one shows any interest in fighting.'

'We will teach them.' Shigong Egg raised his wings and placed them behind his back. 'Do not fear, Professor Rooster. Fighting is not the only skill required for combat. We shall make warriors of them all.'

'So you really think you can do it?' Professor Rooster repeated the question.

'Of course.' Shigong Egg's head met the floor. Slowly he raised his other foot off the ground so he was doing a perfect headstand.

'Very well.' Professor Rooster rose stiffly from his chair. He limped towards the door.

'Remember, Professor,' Shigong Egg called after him. 'Your faith will be rewarded. This elite combat squad will be capable of any mission you choose to send it on once I have finished with it. The chickens will prevail against your enemies.'

Professor Rooster bowed. 'Then I request that you send for them at once,' he said.

Chapter One

'Who are you calling fat, goose-face?'

At Perrin's Farm a fluffy-looking chicken with puffs of grey feathers around its tummy, a small head and very red cheeks was circling a large goose.

'Forget it, Amy,' another chicken called. 'He's not worth it. Come and play in the barn with us.'

'Yeah,' the goose taunted. 'You heard what your friend said. Now beak it.'

Amy held her ground. 'No one calls me fat and gets away with it,' she hissed.

'All right,' the goose honked, looking down at her. 'Let's say you're tubby instead.'

'They're just feathers!' Amy ruffled her tummy fluff. Her cheeks glowed. 'I'm not tubby. And even if I was, there's no reason to be rude about it. Now apologise, or else.'

'I'm not apologising to some kid chicken,' the goose sneered.

'Fine,' Amy muttered. 'Don't say I didn't warn you.' She glanced at the barn floor. It was filthy. Perfect for what she had in mind. She squatted down, gave a little wriggle, then launched herself at the goose and knocked him to the ground. The goose lay on his back, his legs in the air. Amy leaped on top of him with a cry and rubbed her tummy in the goose's face.

'What move do you call that, Amy?' one of the other chickens shouted.

'The feather dusty!' Amy shouted back.

'Amy!' It was her mother. She sounded cross.

Amy sighed. She scrambled away from the goose. 'See you later, guys.' She waved goodbye to her friends and trailed after her mother into the coop. She was surprised to see her father was there too. He was normally out practising his crowing at this time in the afternoon.

'She was wrestling,' her mother said. 'Again! With a goose this time.'

'That's the third time this month you've got into a fight,' her father commented.

'It wasn't my fault!' Amy protested. 'He called me tubby! I asked him to apologise and he wouldn't.'

Her parents glanced at one another.

'Amy,' her mother said, 'your father and I had a letter this morning by pigeon post.' She paused. 'About you.'

'Me?' Amy said in astonishment.

'Here.' Her father held it out to her. 'I think you should read it.'

Amy took the envelope. It bore a strange postmark with a picture of mountains on it. She pulled out the letter.

International School of Kung Fu for Poultry (KFP)
High in the Mountains
Tibet

TO THE PARENTS OR GUARDIANS OF MISS AMY CLUCKBUCKET

Your daughter has been selected to attend an advanced training course as part of an elite combat squad of young chickens.

Special skill: Courage

Signed Shigong-Egg
Highest bird of Martial Arts

Amy turned the letter over. On the reverse side were instructions about how to get there by albatross.

There was silence for a moment.

'Seeing how it's nearly time for you to fly the coop . . .' her mother began.

'And how much you like wrestling . . .' her father added.

'We think it would be a good idea . . .' her mother continued.

'To accept,' her father finished.

'You mean I can go?' Amy could hardly contain her excitement. This was the sort of adventure she craved. She'd been praying for this all her young chicken life.

'If it's what you want.' Her mother gave her a hug.

'Of course it is!'

'We'd better be quick,' her father smiled. 'The flight leaves tonight.'

Ten days later the albatross finally put down in the snowy courtyard at KFP. Amy slid off its back and said thank you like her mother had taught her. It had been a long, long flight: the albatross covering nearly five hundred miles every day. Amy could fly – sort of. But it took a lot of flapping and squawking to get airborne, and she couldn't go very high before she got tired and had to come down again or rest in a tree until she got her breath back. She wished she could fly like the albatross. Maybe that was one of the things she would learn at her new school.

Amy waved as the albatross took off. She watched until it was out of sight, then scuttled up the steps to the big wooden door of the monastery and pressed the bell.

A tall bird with a red headband opened a hatch at the bottom of the door. 'Welcome,' he said. 'Please come in and meet your fellow chicken warriors.'

Amy hopped through the hatch and followed the bird along a stone passageway. The monastery was very quiet. She wondered where all the other students were.

5

'It is rest time,' the bird said, as if reading her thoughts.

'Oh good.' Amy liked resting, especially on a comfy pile of straw. If that was part of the training, she thought she'd be pretty good at being a chicken warrior.

The bird headed left along another passageway. Amy trotted after him, feeling puffed out. The bird had very long legs and she had very short ones. She hoped it wasn't too much further.

'Here is your dormitory.' The bird stopped in front of another door. 'Dinner is at six.' He disappeared back along the passageway.

Amy felt nervous. It was like going to school for the first time. What if the other chickens didn't like her? What if they had already made friends? But then she couldn't very well stand out in the passageway until dinner time. Telling herself not to be silly, she took a deep breath, pushed open the hatch and stepped inside.

The dormitory was a small oblong room with a stone floor. Along each of the three walls was a

pallet of straw. Amy saw immediately that none of the pallets was occupied by resting chickens. On the contrary, the two chickens in the room were very busy doing something else altogether.

In one corner a white chicken with looping black tail feathers, a grey scarf and spectacles was putting the finishing touches to some sort of machine with a spanner.

And in the other corner a beautiful chicken with glossy, honey-coloured feathers was practising backflips.

Amy stared at the honey-coloured chicken in admiration. It wasn't just the backflips that impressed her. Or even the pretty purple ribbon pinned to the beautiful chicken's chest. It was her legs! Most chickens, like Amy, had scrawny pink legs. This chicken had brown feathery boots all the way down to her elegant toes.

As soon as they saw Amy, the two chickens stopped what they were doing.

'Hello,' the honey-coloured one said. 'I'm Boo.'

'And I'm Ruth,' the white chicken said. She

adjusted her spectacles. 'You must be Amy.'

Amy nodded. She suddenly felt very shy. These chickens were so cool. She wasn't sure if they'd want to hang out with her.

She needn't have worried. Boo put her wing around Amy's shoulder and steered her towards one of the straw pallets. 'This one's yours,' she said. 'I'm in the one opposite. Ruth bagged the best bed by the window.'

'I was here first!' Ruth protested. 'And anyway, I need the light for making my inventions.'

'Your inventions?' Amy repeated, bouncing up and down on the straw.

'Ruth's very brainy,' Boo explained. 'That's why she's here. Special skill: Intelligence. That's what her invitation said. She's always inventing things, aren't you, Ruth?'

'Well . . .' Ruth said modestly.

'So you both got invitations to train for the elite combat squad too?' Amy had brought her letter with her just in case she needed it. Her mother had rolled it up carefully, wrapped it in a bit of

polythene bag, and tied it round Amy's neck with a piece of string. Amy pulled it off to show to the others. She unwrapped the letter and spread it out on the floor.

'Mine was exactly the same,' Boo said, reading it carefully, 'except for the special skill.'

'And mine,' Ruth confirmed.

'What's your special skill, Boo?' Amy asked.

'Perseverance,' Boo said.

'Per-see-what?' said Amy.

'Perseverance,' Boo laughed.

'It means being determined and not giving up,' Ruth explained.

'Oh,' Amy felt awkward. It was the sort of thing she probably should have known. She wished she'd paid more attention in English.

'Don't worry, Amy,' Boo said quickly. 'I didn't know what it was either until Ruth told me. I just have it naturally because if I didn't I wouldn't be any good at gymnastics. You've got to keep trying or you never get any better.' She gave Amy's wing a little squeeze.

Amy felt reassured. She smiled at Boo. 'Is that what you got the ribbon for?' she asked. 'Gymnastics?'

'Yes,' Boo nodded. 'Purple's my favourite colour,' she added. 'I won't wear anything else.'

'Your strength is courage,' Ruth said, reading from Amy's letter. 'That's really impressive. Boo and I are completely useless when it comes to a fight. We keep getting into trouble from the instructors here for chickening out. It'll be brilliant having you on the team.'

'Thank you, Ruth,' Amy felt pleased. She really liked her new friends. This was going to be fun.

'So what sort of fighting do you do, Amy?' Boo asked.

'Wrestling mostly,' Amy told her. 'But only when someone's being mean,' she added hastily, in case Boo thought she picked fights for no reason.

'The question is,' Ruth said slowly, 'why are we here? I mean why has Shigong Egg decided to train up an elite combat squad of chickens? There must be something he wants us to do. You don't have any idea what it is, do you, Amy?'

Amy shook her head. 'None at all.' Actually, she hadn't really thought about it before. It was a good question.

'And why us?' Ruth continued. 'I mean we're much younger than most of the birds who come here to train.'

'Stop worrying, Ruth,' Boo said. 'I'm sure that nut-job emu will tell us what he wants when we've completed the training.'

'What nut-job emu?' Amy asked.

'She means Shigong Egg,' Ruth said. 'Highest Bird of Martial Arts: Master of KFP – he's the one who sent the letters.' She giggled. 'Wait till you meet him. Nothing he says makes any sense. And he smells like an old duster.'

'He's really bendy though,' Boo conceded. 'Until I got here, he was the only bird on the planet who could do the Ou-Jay leg-neck knot.'

'What on earth's that?' Amy asked, bewildered.

'I'll show you after dinner,' Boo promised. 'Right now Ruth needs a volunteer to try out her latest invention. Do you want to have a go?'

'Okay,' said Amy. She scuttled over to the machine. 'What is it?'

'A poo-powered poultry projector,' Ruth said proudly. 'It's to help birds who can't fly very well fly better. Birds like me,' she added ruefully.

'And me,' Boo said.

'And me,' Amy admitted. She was secretly glad that Boo and Ruth weren't any better at flying than she was. They seemed to be so good at everything else. She stood patiently while Ruth placed the contraption on her back and clipped the straps together under her wings.

'Chin up!' Ruth ordered.

Amy lifted her chin as Ruth pulled the helmet down over her head.

Amy heard a buzzing sound.

'It's working!' Ruth cried. 'It's picking up your thought processes. All you have to do is imagine you're airborne and the machine will do the rest.'

'Go on, Amy,' Boo encouraged. 'You can do it.'

Amy closed her eyes and stretched out her wings. She tried to imagine what it was like to be the

albatross. Slowly she rose into the air. *This is brilliant*, she thought. *I'm not even flapping.*

Suddenly the machine made a rude noise.

Amy returned to the dormitory floor with a thud.

'Are you all right?' Boo helped her up.

Amy nodded. 'I'm fine.' She slid out of the straps and removed the helmet. 'I hope I didn't break your machine,' she said worriedly.

'I don't think so.' Ruth examined it. 'Flip!' she exclaimed. 'We ran out of poo. That's why it didn't work. I'll have to think of a way of storing more fuel.'

'What about using fart gas instead?' Boo suggested.

'No!' Ruth said impatiently. 'I need the fart gas for the rotten-egg stink bomb.'

'Oh yes, of course!' Boo glanced at Amy and raised her eyebrows. 'Silly me!'

Amy giggled. Boo was funny. And Ruth didn't seem to mind the joke. She was grinning too.

Just then a strange bonging noise came from somewhere below.

'What's that?' Amy asked in alarm.

'It's the dinner gong,' Boo told her. 'Come on. Let's get down there before the turkeys eat all the grubs.'

The three chickens hopped out of the hatch and raced down the corridor towards the dining room, squawking and chattering at the tops of their lungs.

Chapter Two

Three weeks later . . .

'I've come to hand in my resignation.'

'So have I.'

Shigong Egg looked up in surprise. Two of his highest ranked martial arts teachers stood in front of him. He took a deep breath. 'Be calm, gentlemen,' he said. 'Do not act in haste. You have many moons to paddle.'

The swans glanced at one another. Shigong Egg was a wise master, but he could talk a lot of rubbish sometimes.

'It's the chickens, Master,' the first swan said. 'They won't cooperate.'

Shigong Egg stared at him without blinking. 'Explain.'

The swan swallowed. Shigong Egg could outstare a snake. 'The small one, Amy, wishes only to wrestle,' he began. 'We've been trying to teach her

Kung Fu moves but her legs are too short to kick properly and she keeps falling over.'

The swans waited. Shigong Egg didn't blink. 'What of the others?' he said eventually.

'The tall one, Ruth,' the first swan answered, 'she's clever but she shows no interest in being a warrior. Yesterday when I attempted to engage her in combat she shot me in the eye with a rotten egg from a rocket launch she'd made out of a cardboard tube and some fart gas.' He shuddered.

Shigong Egg went into a backbend. His head re-emerged between his legs. He was still staring.

'The one called Boo, she has perfect balance,' the second swan said, 'but she doesn't want to get her boots dirty and she won't fight. And she's even demanding that we give her a purple silk headband, Master, even though we told her you were the only one worthy of such an honour.'

'Ah,' Shigong Egg muttered, 'my purple silk headband. I wonder . . .' He straightened up. 'Do not speak more of resigning. Your work is done. Now go in peace!'

The swans bowed. They shuffled out. Shigong Egg still hadn't blinked. He rang a bell. His servant entered. 'Green tea, Master?' the servant asked.

'Green is the colour of grass,' Shigong Egg observed. 'As well as trees, peas, teas and mouldy cheese.'

'Indeed, Master,' the servant agreed. He poured the tea.

'It is time to test what our young chickens have learned, Menial,' Shigong Egg finally blinked slowly, one eye after the other. 'I intend to set them a task.'

'What level task, Master?' the servant enquired with interest. There were forty-nine levels of task. One was the easiest. Forty-nine was the hardest. Only Shigong Egg had completed them all.

'Level fifty,' Shigong Egg replied.

The servant gasped. He'd forgotten about level fifty. 'But, Master,' he whispered. 'The yeti . . .'

'Do not worry, Menial,' Shigong Egg closed his eyes. 'It takes many steps to reach the top floor . . . unless you take the lift.'

'Wise words indeed, Master,' the servant said. 'But . . .'

'ENOUGH!' Shigong Egg thundered. 'Get the chickens. My mind is made up.'

The next day Amy, Boo and Ruth trudged out of the monastery gates into the snow and headed towards a track that led deep into the mountains.

'Remember,' Shigong Egg called after them, 'you must know your enemy in order to defeat him.'

The three chickens exchanged glances.

'What's he talking about now?' Ruth muttered.

Shigong Egg raised one foot off the ground. 'The road to wisdom lies through sheep dung . . . *sheep dung . . . sheep dung . . .*' His voice echoed round the mountains.

'Sure!' Amy giggled. Treading in sheep dung didn't make you wise. If it did she'd be a chicken genius by now, like Ruth, after all the sheep dung she'd trodden in at the farm.

'Good luck!' The swans circled overhead, sniggering.

'Why are they looking so cheerful?' Amy asked.

'Probably because we're going to die,' Boo said mournfully.

'It can't be that hard!' Amy said brightly.

'Weren't you listening, Amy?' Ruth sounded

astonished. 'Didn't you hear what that nut-job emu wants us to do?'

'Yeah,' Amy replied. 'He wants us to trek up the mountain to the yeti's lair and steal back the purple silk headband the yeti stole from him. So what?'

'Do you actually know what a yeti is, Amy?' Boo asked gently.

'Not really,' Amy admitted.

Boo sighed. 'You tell her,' she said to Ruth.

'The yeti, also known as Bigfoot or the Abominable Snowman is a legendary creature similar to a bear,' Ruth explained. 'It is believed to inhabit caves, is approximately two metres tall, is covered in thick white fur and has a large appetite for fresh meat, especially chicken.'

'Oh,' said Amy, impressed. 'How do you know all that?'

'I found a book in the library,' Ruth said. 'I brought it with me if you want to have a look. It's called *The Habits of Yetis.*'

'Maybe later.' Amy didn't think she'd be able to see a book; the weather was getting so bad. She

glanced back. The monastery was out of sight. The swans had disappeared. The snow came in thick swirls. It was turning into a blizzard. She was smaller than the others. Her tummy feathers were wet from rubbing in the snow. 'Are we nearly there yet?' she asked plaintively.

'I don't think so,' Ruth said, glancing about. 'But we'd better find shelter before this gets any worse.' The wind whistled past them, pushing the snow into drifts around their ankles.

'What about over there?' Amy suggested. She pointed to the mouth of a great cave, which led into the rocky mountainside.

'Are you sure that isn't where the yeti lives?' Boo asked.

Ruth shook her head. 'The swans said it lives on the other side of the mountain.'

'Well, come on then, what are we waiting for? Let's go.' Amy took a step towards the cave and sank up to her tail.

Boo held out a wing towards her. 'Grab hold. I'll give you a pull,' she offered.

Amy grabbed Boo's wing gratefully. Boo was really strong. Amy felt herself being lifted out of the snowdrift. She dusted herself off.

BOOM!

'What was that?' Boo shouted.

'It came from up there,' Amy said, looking fearfully towards the mountaintop.

The snow was getting even heavier. In fact huge great chunks of it were falling all around them.

Ruth blinked at the tumbling blocks of snow. 'Quick!' she shouted. 'It's an avalanche!'

The chickens struggled towards the cave entrance and threw themselves in. They huddled together.

CRASH!

A wall of snow cascaded past the mouth of the cave. They were just in time!

'We may have to spend the night here,' Ruth said. 'And wait for this storm to blow over.'

'Oh well, look on the bright side,' Amy said. Looking on the bright side was something her mother had always taught her to do. 'At least it's dry!' She chucked down her backpack and shook

her wet feathers. The cave felt warm and cosy, like the coop at Perrin's Farm. 'And we're safe from the yeti.'

Ruth had brought a huge backpack with her. She threw it on the floor and pulled out her library book. 'I'm going to find out more about the yeti,' she said. 'You two can go and explore if you like.' She started to read.

'Shall we try and find some bedding?' Amy suggested to Boo. 'Then we can have a snack.' The chickens had been given some mealworm and seeds to take with them as emergency rations before they left the monastery.

'Okay,' Boo agreed. 'There's none in here though. What about through there?' She pointed to an opening at the back of the cave.

Amy scuttled over and peered through it. 'There's another cave,' she said. 'They must go right under the mountain.' She sniffed. 'I can smell hay.' The scent reminded her of Perrin's Farm at harvest time. She took another sniff. 'And something that whiffs a lot like sheep dung.' She scratched her head. *That was odd. Hadn't Shigong Egg said something about sheep dung?*

Boo joined her. 'You go first,' she said. 'I don't like the dark.'

Amy didn't like the dark either. But she knew she had to be brave for Boo's sake. Boo looked really scared. 'Okay.' She crept through the opening. Then she stopped in surprise. 'Look, Boo!' she exclaimed. 'Someone's lit a fire!'

In the corner of the second cave a log fire crackled merrily, radiating warmth and casting a red glow around the rock.

'Thank goodness. I'm freezing!' Boo ran towards the fire and sat down. She shook the snow from her boots and started to preen her shiny feathers.

Amy scuttled over to join her. Food was roasting on a spit above the flames. Amy couldn't make out what it was. The food wasn't long and thin like worms. It wasn't round and flat like beetles either. It didn't even look like a vegetable or a piece of fruit. It was thick and chunky, with two bits sticking out on either side, one longer than the other. 'I wonder who lives here?' she said, looking round the cave curiously. A little way away from the fire was a large pile of straw. Amy hopped on to it and made herself comfortable. She felt drowsy. She normally went to bed at dusk and the warmth of the fire in the dark cave was making her sleepy. She closed her eyes.

'Grrrrrrrr.'

'What was that?' Boo whispered.

Amy opened her eyes.

'My stomach, probably,' she yawned. 'I'm starving.'

'Grrrrrrrr.' The noise came again.

Amy listened closely. It wasn't her stomach that was growling, she decided. And it couldn't be Ruth who was making the noise because it was coming from the wrong direction. The growling came from somewhere deep within the mountain: from further inside the system of caves.

'It sounds more like a bear,' Boo hissed.

'Didn't Ruth say the yeti was a bit like a bear?' Amy remarked. She felt proud of herself for remembering. She was learning loads more stuff at

KFP than she ever had at her old school.

Boo stared at the roasting food. Then she stared at the pile of straw. 'Flap!' she squawked. 'It's the yeti! Budge over.' Amy made room for her.

Boo burrowed her way under the straw. 'What are you doing, Amy?' Boo poked her head out. 'Why aren't you hiding?'

'I'm not scared of the yeti,' Amy said bravely. 'And anyway, we've got to get the headband off it and take it back to Shigong Egg, remember?'

'Don't be daft,' Boo told her firmly. 'The yeti's about two hundred times the size of you. You can't just grab it off him. We'll have to get back to the entrance and alert Ruth. She's the clever one: she'll think of a plan. If we survive that long, that is.'

'Okay.' Amy burrowed down next to Boo. The two chickens huddled together in a ball of feathers and waited.

Chapter Three

The yeti lumbered into the cave. It was carrying some logs.

'Look!' Amy nudged Boo. 'Shigong Egg's purple silk headband.' The band was tied lopsidedly around the yeti's forehead.

'Never mind that now!' Boo was shivering with fear. 'Please, Amy. Just leave it.'

'All right.' Amy huddled closer to make Boo feel better.

The yeti bent down in front of the fire. It placed the logs on the flames and blew on them until they crackled. Then it removed the spit. Amy watched in horror as its sharp teeth began to tear at the roasted meat.

'Mmm, rabbit!' it grunted. 'Me like.' It took another mouthful. 'But not as much as chicken.'

Amy gulped. No wonder the cooking had two bits sticking out either side. It was meat. Those were the rabbit's legs!

'What are we going to do?' Boo hissed. 'I don't want to be eaten by a yeti!'

'It won't eat us,' Amy said soothingly. 'It doesn't know we're here.'

The yeti finished its meal. 'Mmm, me sleepy,' it said. 'Me want nap.' It strolled towards the pile of straw, yawning and stretching.

'Now it's going to squash us instead!' Boo moaned.

Amy racked her brain. They had to do something! Ruth was nowhere to be seen. She was probably too absorbed in her book to realise that there was a real, live yeti in the next-door cave! Amy would have to think of a plan to get them out of there herself. And she hadn't given up on the headband either, whatever Boo said. There *must* be a way. She wondered what Shigong Egg would do.

Suddenly she had an idea. 'Come on, Boo.' She dragged Boo backwards out of the straw so that they were behind the pile where the yeti couldn't see them. 'You distract it with the Ou-jay leg-neck knot. I'll get the headband. Then we'll make a run for it. I'll be back in a minute.' She scuttled off.

'What?' Boo squawked. 'Are you joking?'

The yeti spied Amy. 'Yum, chicken!' it said.

'Boo! Do it now!' Amy screeched.

Boo edged out from behind the pile of straw. 'Yoo-hoo!' she called in a strangled voice.

The yeti turned round and shuffled towards her.

Boo didn't move.

'Boo!' Amy shrieked. 'What are you waiting for? Do it!'

'I can't remember how!' Boo sobbed.

'Yes, you can.' Amy stopped in her tracks.

'I can't!' Boo wailed.

'But I've seen you!' Amy said. 'You did it in the dormitory.'

'That was when it didn't matter!' Boo howled. 'I'm too scared!'

'Come on, Boo,' Amy urged. 'I know you can do it. That's your skill, remember: perseverance. Just for a few seconds. I'll be there in a tick.'

Amy could see Boo hesitate. Then, to her relief, Boo took a deep breath and lifted one leg off the floor.

The yeti stopped. 'Funny chicken,' it said.

'That's it, Boo! Keep going!' Amy darted about in the shadows, keeping one eye on Boo. Boo's leg kept travelling upwards. Her toes crept one by one around her neck. Any minute now and they would reach her knee.

'Ooohhhh!' The yeti watched, fascinated.

'Good work, Boo!' Amy had found what she wanted – a patch of dirt. She dipped down and coated her tummy fluff in muck. *Now for the feather dusty!* With any luck she would catch the yeti off guard long enough for her to get the headband. She ran round in a circle, flapping her wings furiously, and took off towards the roof of the cave.

The yeti was still watching Boo. 'Me like!' it grunted, clapping its paws. 'Funny chicken.'

Boo slid her shin under her thigh.

Amy got ready to feather dusty the yeti. She did one more loop of the cave ceiling and locked on to her target. Any minute now . . .

Suddenly there was a shout from behind her. Amy looked round. It was Ruth! She was wearing the poo-powered poultry projector. She must have

brought it with her in her backpack!

'Don't worry, guys! I'm on it!' Ruth cried. 'Let Operation Remove Headband commence.' She rammed the projector helmet on to her head and began to lift into the air.

'Ruth!' Amy squawked. 'Don't! Boo and I have got it covered!'

Ruth appeared not to have heard her. She was struggling with the helmet. 'Barn it!' Ruth swore. 'It's slipped!' She tried to adjust the straps. 'Help! I can't see where I'm going!'

'Watch out!' Amy yelled. Ruth zigzagged towards her.

THONK!

Ruth hurtled into Amy.

Amy plummeted on to Boo.

Boo crashed to the floor.

The poo-powered poultry projector made a rude noise.

'Mayday! Mayday! I've run out of poo!' Ruth shouted. She spiralled downwards and landed on the others.

The yeti came out of its trance. 'Lots of chicken!' it said, licking its lips. 'Yum!'

'Help!' Boo shrieked.

'Can someone give me a hand with this helmet?' The helmet was still jammed over Ruth's eyes. 'I can't see a thing!'

Amy tried to stay calm. 'Ruth!' she squawked,

yanking at the helmet. 'What else have you got in that backpack of yours?'

'I think the rotten-egg stink bomb's in there somewhere,' Ruth said. 'Why?'

Amy tugged at the helmet. It shot off Ruth's head. 'That's why!' she said, pointing at the yeti. It was only feet away from them. 'Run!' she yelled. 'I'm going for the stink bomb.'

Amy lowered her head and ran as fast as she could between the yeti's legs. The yeti made a grab for her but Amy dodged him. She raced into the first cave and tipped up Ruth's backpack. The rotten-egg stink bomb tumbled on to the floor. Amy grabbed it.

'Quick, Amy!' Ruth yelled. 'The yeti's got Boo!'

Amy ran as fast as she could back to her friends, her little legs aching with the effort.

'Hold on, Boo!'

The yeti had Boo in one big hairy hand. With the other it stoked the fire with a stick. 'Yummy chicken,' it said.

'Here!' Amy gave the stink bomb to Ruth.

Ruth pressed a button.

WHOOSH! A cloud of evil-smelling gas enveloped the cave.

The yeti staggered backwards. 'Yuck! Fart gas,' it grumbled. 'Me no like.' It dropped Boo on the pile of straw.

'Are you all right?' Amy ran to her.

Boo looked dazed. 'I think so,' she said.

'Give it another blast, Ruth!' Amy yelled.

WHOOSH! A second cloud of gas shot out of the cardboard tube.

The yeti removed Shigong Egg's purple silk headband from around his forehead and held it to his nose.

'Drop the headband!' Ruth shouted. 'Or I'll hit you with a rotten egg.'

The yeti hesitated.

'Okay, you've asked for it!'

SPLAT! The egg hurtled towards the yeti and smashed in its eye.

The yeti howled in anguish. He dabbed at the putrid egg with the purple silk headband.

'Oh dear!' said Ruth. 'That wasn't part of the plan.'

'Drop it!' Amy ordered the yeti. 'Or you'll get another egg in the face.'

The yeti had had enough. It dropped the headband on the ground and shambled out of the cave through the opening in the rock from which it had come. 'GGGGRRRRrrrrrrrrrrrrrr . . .' Its grumbling became quieter as it disappeared into the bowels of the mountain.

'It's gone!' Boo whispered.

'We did it!' Ruth threw herself on to the pile of straw. She lay on her back with her legs in the air.

'Well, sort of.' Amy slipped off the hay and collected the headband. It didn't look very clean. And it certainly didn't smell very nice. She couldn't imagine Shigong Egg would want to wear it again.

'That was the most terrifying thing I've ever done in my life,' Boo said, rolling on her back and sticking her legs in the air like Ruth.

'Me too,' Amy jumped back on to the straw with her friends and did the same.

The three chickens stared up at the roof of the cave. There was silence for a few minutes.

'Do you think we should tell Shigong Egg about what happened?' Ruth asked eventually. 'I mean about me crashing into Amy with the poo-powered poultry projector and Boo nearly getting eaten by the yeti?'

'No,' said Amy confidently. 'He doesn't need to know all that. He'll just be happy we got his headband back. Even if it is a bit smelly.'

'The thing is,' said Boo slowly, 'I don't know if I'm really cut out for being a chicken warrior. It's too scary.'

'Of course you are,' Amy reassured her. 'You were brilliant.' She giggled. 'We had that yeti licked until Ruth crashed into me.'

'Yeah, sorry about that,' Ruth said. 'I need to sort out that helmet. Just as well I brought the stink bomb too.'

'That was really clever of you,' Amy admitted.

'And you were incredibly brave, Amy,' Boo said.

'Thanks.' Amy rolled off the straw. 'Now let's get

back to KFP and see what that nut-job emu has in store for us next.'

'Congratulations!' Back at the monastery Shigong Egg handed them each a certificate in exchange for his purple silk headband, which he handed to his servant to wash.

Amy glanced at hers with pride.

THIS IS TO CERTIFY THAT
Amy Cluckbucket
HAS PASSED THE KFP ELITE TRAINING CAMP
WITH DISTINCTION FOR COURAGE

Ruth got one for intelligence and Boo for perseverance.

'It is time for the next stage of your journey,' Shigong Egg said.

'You mean we're not staying here?' Amy was stunned. Surely he wasn't going to send them home?

'Your training is complete,' Shigong Egg told her. 'Now you must meet your employer. I have contacted your parents and guardians to inform them.'

Amy looked at him, wide eyed. *Employer!* That sounded really grown up. She wondered who it could be.

Shigong Egg clapped his wings. 'Menial, tell Professor Emeritus Rooster that his elite combat squad is ready for action. It is time to send them to Chicken HQ.'

Chapter Four

'Are we nearly there yet?' Amy said for the umpteenth time. It seemed even further coming back from Tibet on the albatross than it had going out. Ruth said it was something to do with the wind direction.

'I think we might be,' Boo said. The albatross was preparing to land.

Amy peered down. A huge park spread out beneath them. A river ran along one edge, sparkling in the sunlight. Beyond the river lay a patchwork of brown and green fields. In the centre of the park stood a great stone manor house, reached by a long drive that snaked from a distant road through the rolling parkland between an avenue of trees. To the north and east, the park was bordered by deep, dark woods, which continued into the distance as far as Amy could see.

Amy blinked. She had never seen anything as big as this park. It was ten times the size of Perrin's

Farm. It dwarfed the International School of Kung Fu for Poultry. She couldn't imagine ever finding her way around such a huge place.

The albatross flew towards the rear of the house. There was another lawn. And several large pens full of lush grass surrounded with chicken wire. Amy glimpsed the red roofs of chicken coops tucked under some trees. It was impossible to tell how many there were.

The albatross flew on. Amy saw a wall of crumbling brick with a green door in the middle of it with the paint peeling off. The albatross flew over the wall. It was a garden, Amy saw, with not just one but four walls and flowerbeds in rows with narrow paths in between them. But the beds were overgrown with weeds and tangles of thick-stemmed plants, which Amy thought might be vegetables. Fruit trees grew around the walls; their thin branches jutting out at all angles from broken trellises, competing for space with dog roses and brambles. There was a smell of rotten apples. The garden looked as if it had been neglected for years.

The albatross circled down. Along one of the four walls stood a series of derelict potting sheds and it was in front of these that the albatross landed.

Amy looked about. There was no sign of Professor Emeritus Rooster. In fact there was no sign of life at all except vegetables and the odd worm. She sniffed. It was a while since they'd had anything to eat. The rotten apples smelled good. Amy slid off the albatross on to the ground. Boo and Ruth followed suit.

'I don't know what I was expecting,' Ruth said. 'But it wasn't this.'

'Let's ask the albatross if he knows where Chicken HQ is,' Amy suggested. She gave the albatross a pat. 'Is this definitely the place?' she asked.

'Definitely,' said the albatross. 'The Potting Sheds, Old Vegetable Garden, Dudley Manor, Dudley Estate, Dudley. That's what I was told. This is the place all right.'

'But which one's Chicken HQ?' Amy wondered.

'Search me.' The albatross got ready to fly off.

'Maybe it's this one,' Boo strode up the path to the first potting shed.

'I'll try the next one,' Ruth said.

'I'll start the other end,' Amy trudged over to the last shed door and turned the handle. 'This one's open!' she shouted excitedly.

'So's this one,' Ruth called.

'This one is too!' Boo said.

Amy frowned. That didn't sound right. The potting sheds couldn't *all* be Chicken HQ! She gave the door a push with her foot. It creaked open. Amy tiptoed in. Inside the shed it was pitch-dark. For some reason the window didn't seem to let in any light. She hopped up on to a table, fumbled for a light switch and flicked it on. A flash of bright light lit up the interior of the shed.

'WOW!' Amy whistled.

'That's amazing!' Ruth breathed.

Amy cocked her head to one side in surprise. It sounded as if Ruth was inside the shed too!

'It's really cool!'

What? So was Boo!

Amy glanced to her left. The other chickens *were* inside. All the potting-shed doors led into the same

43

place. It *was* all Chicken HQ! She looked around in amazement. The potting sheds had been joined together to form a control centre. At one end were the chickens' sleeping quarters. At the other end was a large cupboard marked 'GADGETS'. And in the middle of the potting sheds, on top of a cardboard box, was an old laptop computer with three garden stools in front of it for the chickens to sit on.

Ruth darted forwards towards the cupboard to inspect the gadgets. 'Wow!' she cried, rummaging about inside. 'There are flight-booster engines. And infra-red super-spec headsets with advanced radar tracking. Bloomin' peck!' she yelled. 'There's even a mite blaster!'

'What's a mite blaster?' Amy asked, mystified.

'It's a bit like my rotten-egg stink bomb only much more powerful,' Ruth explained. 'And instead of rotten eggs it blasts out mites.'

'That sounds itchy,' Amy said. She'd had mites once when she was a chick and it wasn't fun at all.

Boo was examining the sleeping quarters. 'There's a straw pallet each that folds up into the wall,' she

said. 'They're operated by a bed-tidy button! And there's a birdbath! It's so cool, Amy, come and see!'

Amy scuttled over. The birdbath even had a hosepipe that fed into it, connected at the other end to a garden tap. Beside the bath lay a small blue packet with a picture of a chicken on the front.

'What's this?' Amy picked up the packet.

'It's Bird Bright,' Ruth told her. 'It makes your feathers shine.' She clasped her wings together in excitement. 'Professor Rooster's thought of everything! I can't wait to use it on my boots!' She began to fill the bath.

Amy was pleased for her friends. Ruth had her gadgets and Boo had her Bird Bright. And with any luck, Amy thought, casting a surreptitious eye at the laptop, *she* had chicken TV. She scuttled over to the computer, switched on the screen and carefully typed in BBC on the keyboard with her toes. BBC, Amy knew from her dad, stood for Bird Broadcasting Corporation. Amy also knew that the BBC was very good at covering sport. She flicked through a few channels until she found the chicken wrestling.

It was ages since she'd seen any. The chickens at Perrin's Farm had managed to rig up an old TV they'd found in the barn, but most of them wanted to watch dance shows, not wrestling. Just occasionally Amy and her dad used to sneak a quick look at it, even though her mum didn't approve. Amy felt a bit sad at the thought of her mum and dad but she consoled herself that now she could see the wrestling whenever she wanted! She settled down to watch.

Just then the screen flickered. A very stern-looking black cockerel with shiny green tail feathers and a scarlet comb appeared. He stared hard at Amy.

Amy felt uncomfortable. It was as if he was looking right at her! 'He can't see me, can he?' Amy whispered.

Boo and Ruth came over to take a look.

'I think he probably can,' Ruth said, examining the screen. 'It looks like it's two-way.'

'Quite right, Ruth,' the cockerel spoke at last. 'I *can* see you. I'm Professor Emeritus Rooster. Welcome to Chicken HQ.'

Chapter Five

The chickens sat on the three stools listening carefully. Amy's heart beat fast. Finally they were going to find out what they had been training for. She hoped it wasn't as difficult as the task Shigong Egg had set them.

'You're probably wondering why you're here,' Professor Rooster said. 'The reason is quite simple. Your mission is to prevent the innocent chickens of Dudley Manor from being murdered by some of the most evil and ferocious predators known to poultry.'

Amy nearly fell off her garden stool. She glanced at the others. Boo and Ruth looked equally stunned. None of them had expected this. The yeti was one thing but *preventing murder*?! That was grown-up stuff.

'The three of you were specially selected by Shigong Egg at my request for this highly dangerous

mission,' Professor Rooster continued. 'It will take courage, intelligence and perseverance if you are to succeed. Above all it will require teamwork.'

'You sure he hasn't got us mixed up with someone else?' Boo whispered.

Amy stole another glance at her. *Poor Boo*, Amy thought. *She looks terrified.* She reached out a wing and gave Boo a pat. Boo didn't respond. She didn't

even seem to notice Amy's kindness. Her feathers trembled.

'I admit you weren't my first choice,' Professor Rooster said. 'I thought it would be better to choose a professional poultry protector rather than three young chickens like you, but Shigong Egg persuaded me otherwise.' He paused. 'I must say I didn't think you had it in you to defeat the yeti. But you proved me wrong. And if you can defeat the yeti, you're ready for action.'

Amy felt herself go crimson. *Professor Rooster didn't know that Boo had got caught, or about the accident with the poo-powered poultry projector.* She exchanged stricken looks with Ruth. 'What shall we do?' she mouthed.

'I don't know,' Ruth mouthed back.

Boo just kept staring at the screen. She seemed to be in some kind of petrified trance.

'It's time to introduce you to the MOST WANTED Club,' Professor Rooster said. 'A collection of the worst criminals known to chickens.'

Amy told herself to keep calm. Nothing could be worse than the yeti.

The screen flickered again. Pictures of a large French poodle with a chef's hat on popped up.

'Kebab Claude,' Professor Rooster said. The camera honed in on the poodle, showing him from every angle. 'This dog will chop you, remove your giblets and turn you into a chicken dinner for one before you can say "pass the gravy". Last attack on our chickens, nine months ago. Six dead. All barbecued. With onions on the side.'

Amy's red cheeks paled.

'Tiny Tony Tiddles.' The next set of pictures flashed on to the screen: this time of a small black and white cat with an evil grin and gangster hat pulled down over his ears. 'He may be small,' Professor Rooster said, 'but he's got a big appetite for chicken. He'll pick you off one at a time if you give him the chance. *Bam. Bam. Bam.* No recent reported sightings but he's still out there somewhere, waiting for his opportunity. He'll be back. You can bet your knobbly knees.'

Amy felt her knobbly knees begin to knock.

'Next up, the Pigeon-Poo Gang.' A trio of beefy grey birds wearing shades appeared on the screen.

'They won't eat us, will they?' Amy asked in a small voice. 'I mean, they're birds like us, right?'

'Right,' Professor Rooster replied, 'and wrong. Just because they're birds it won't stop them killing you if you get in the way of their quest for grain. They're traitors. They've crossed to the dark side. So don't be fooled. These are some of the greediest, grottiest gangsters I've ever come across on the Dudley Estate. And if you don't believe me, look at this.' Another picture flashed up. A beak and a pair of legs poked out from under a pile of pigeon sludge. The body was barely recognisable as a chicken.

Amy felt sick.

'Is that it?' Ruth croaked.

Professor Rooster's face appeared on the screen. His comb twitched. 'No,' he said shortly. 'That isn't it. The most MOST WANTED criminal of all is this fiend. The leader of the MOST WANTED Club.'

The screen uploaded a new picture.

52

Amy gave a little scream.

A face leered at her. It had rusty red ears, long whiskers, a pointed nose and a sly grinning mouth full of vicious teeth. Its cunning yellow eyes seemed to be looking straight at her.

'Thaddeus E. Fox,' Professor Rooster's voice trembled. 'Scientific name *Vulpes vulpes*, or red fox. A ruthless murderer who kills chickens not for food, but for fun.'

More pictures flashed up. Thaddeus E. Fox in a top hat, tails and a silk waistcoat, clutching a silver-topped cane in one hand and a decapitated chicken in the other. Thaddeus E. Fox relaxing on a sunbed beside a pond full of dead ducks. Thaddeus E. Fox lying on a picnic blanket beside a hamper full of champagne and Coronation Chicken.

'Educated at Eat'em College for Gentlemen Foxes, Thaddeus E. Fox has led a life of privilege and luxury,' Professor Rooster said. 'But his pretend good manners are just a front. He is a bloodthirsty villain who will stop at nothing to satisfy his lust for poultry. This is all that was left after his last raid.'

53

A video of a crime scene started rolling. It showed a comfortable-looking coop: or at least what must have been a comfortable-looking coop before Thaddeus E. Fox struck. Everything had been destroyed. An empty cot rocked in the corner. A picture of a pretty chicken with blue-coloured wings lay broken on the floor.

Professor Rooster reappeared on the screen. His face was haggard.

'There were several attacks before this one. Each time I did my best to alert the humans. Eventually they strengthened the pens, since when there have been no more chicken deaths. But we can't rely on the humans to look after us. It's only a matter of time before Thaddeus E. Fox and his friends try again, which is why I hired you,' he said. 'So, chickens, you can see what you're up against. I suggest you familiarise yourself with your new surroundings quickly. Our enemies are gathering even as we speak in the Deep Dark Woods. When they strike you must be ready. The chickens of Dudley Manor are relying on you.'

His face fizzled away. The screen went black.

The chickens sat in silence for a few minutes.

'Boo?' Amy said. 'Are you okay?'

'Not really,' Boo shook her head. 'I don't think I can do this. I told you, I'm just not cut out for it. I mean *murder* . . .' Her voice trailed away.

'Me neither,' said Ruth. 'I don't like blood.'

This time Amy didn't say anything. She wasn't sure if she was cut out for it either. She knew she definitely wouldn't be if the others didn't want to do it.

Ruth shuddered. 'Who were those poor chickens anyway?'

'I don't know. Even Professor Rooster looked shocked,' Boo said.

'It wasn't just shock,' Amy said. 'It was something more. Like they were his family or something.'

'Let's check.' Ruth sat down at the computer. Within seconds she'd found what she was looking for. 'You're right, Amy,' she said, pointing at the computer screen. 'They were.'

Amy peered at the screen. It was a newspaper

report from *The Daily Snail* dated nine months previously.

The chickens stared at it in horror.

There was silence for a moment.

'What are we going to do?' Boo said eventually.

'Well . . .' Ruth hesitated. 'I guess it's up to Amy. I mean she's the brave one.'

Amy realised that both her friends were looking at her, waiting for her to speak. She took a deep breath. 'We've come this far,' she said. 'And Professor Rooster's relying on us. I say we give it a try.'

Chapter Six

Down in a burrow in the Deep Dark Woods, Thaddeus E. Fox drew back his chair and stood up. It was time to address the meeting.

He banged his silver cane on the table.

'Friends,' he said. 'Welcome to this session of the MOST WANTED Club.' He surveyed the group. Everyone was present. Tiny Tony Tiddles was there. So were Kebab Claude and the Pigeon-Poo Gang. Kebab Claude had brought his barbecue utensil set along. Thaddeus E. Fox smiled. That was always a good sign. Kebab Claude meant business. Between them they were guaranteed to come up with some seriously evil plotting.

'There are two items on the agenda today.' He handed round some bits of paper.

AGENDA
1. Catching chicken
2. Catching more chicken

He waited patiently while everyone read it. 'We'll start with item one. Claude, do you have any suggestions of where to find our next chicken victims?'

Kebab Claude shrugged. 'Ze problem, Thaddeus, is we 'ave eaten all ze chickens in ze area, except for ze ones at Dudley Manor,' he said.

'Hmm.' Thaddeus E. Fox turned to Tiny Tony Tiddles. 'Tony? Have you sniffed out any chickens recently?'

'Nah,' Tony Tiddles growled. 'Claude's right. We've already hit all the farms. It's Dudley Manor or nowhere.'

'What about the town?' Thaddeus E. Fox asked the Pigeon-Poo Gang. 'Back gardens. Petting zoos. That kind of thing. You know, *urban* chickens.'

'Too much competition,' the leader of the Pigeon-Poo Gang cooed. 'There are foxes queuing up to eat them. They're moving into the town in droves.'

'Pity,' Thaddeus E. Fox snarled. 'Well, gentlemen, it seems we have no choice. Dudley Manor it is. Obviously it won't be as easy as before, since the

60

humans have strengthened the wire around the pens. And they might still be on the lookout for us. We'll have to think outside the coop. Anyone got any ideas?'

Everyone put their paws up, except the Pigeon-Poo Gang, who put their wings up.

'Good!' Thaddeus E. Fox licked his lips. 'Let's hear what you've got. Claude, you go first.'

'I was up at ze Manor zis morning snooping around,' Claude Kebab said, 'and I saw a sign for ze country fair. Zere is a competition for ze best chicken . . .' Kebab Claude paused to wipe a glob of drool from his chops. 'Ze chickens will be in a temporary pen in a different part of ze park. It will be easy for zem to get out wizout ze humans noticing.' He whipped out a spatula. 'And I was thinking, 'ow about a nice barbecue to tempt zem?' He told the gang his plan.

Thaddeus E. Fox nodded approvingly. 'Very good, Claude. Very good.' He licked his lips. 'I'll take my chicken with extra barbecue sauce.'

BRRRIIIIINNNNNGGGG!

On Saturday morning at first light the alarm went off at Chicken HQ.

Amy groped her way out of bed. 'It's Professor Rooster!' she shouted. 'He's on the computer.' She scuttled across the potting shed to her garden stool, trailing wisps of hay between her toes. 'Come on, you two!'

'I need to preen my boots!' Boo complained.

'I can't find my glasses!' Ruth said.

Amy could hear Ruth banging about, knocking into things.

'Good morning, Amy,' Professor Rooster said. 'Where are the others?'

'Practising Kung Fu,' Amy lied. 'They'll be here in a minute.' She didn't want Boo and Ruth to get into trouble with the professor.

'Good.' Professor Rooster said. 'Now listen closely. It's time for your first mission. I've received information from my spies in the Deep Dark Woods that Kebab Claude is planning to set up a worm-burger stand at the Dudley Manor Country

Fair today. All our chickens will be at the fair, as indeed will many others from across the county.' The professor spoke sternly. 'The humans are naive enough to think that Fox and his cronies won't attack in broad daylight or in their presence, but we know better. Claude's plan is to lure unsuspecting chickens out of the pen to his worm-burger stand and grill them for his pals at Fox's burrow. Your mission is to stop him before anyone gets hurt. Good luck.'

Professor Rooster disappeared.

Ruth was the first to react. 'Amy,' she said, 'get the flight-booster engines from the gadget cupboard, will you? Oh, and the super-spec headsets.'

'Okay!' Amy hurried over to the cupboard. Seconds later she returned, wheeling the equipment in a small barrow. 'Wait,' she said, 'shouldn't we take the mite blaster?'

'Good plan,' Ruth agreed. 'We can blast Kebab when he sets up the burger stand. With all that curly fur, he'll be scratching for weeks! Let's go.'

'Wait, where's Boo?' Amy said.

'I'm in here!' There was a loud knocking from

behind the wall in the chickens' sleeping quarters. 'Some idiot pressed the bed-tidy button.'

'That was me,' Ruth admitted. 'I was looking for my glasses. Sorry.'

'I'll get her.' Amy went to rescue Boo while Ruth got the mite blaster.

Eventually, after a lot of squawking and flapping, the chickens were ready for action. They donned their super-spec headsets. Then they strapped on the flight-booster engines, dashed out of Chicken HQ and took off into the sky.

ZOOM! They zipped over the garden wall. The flight-booster engines really worked. Amy didn't seem to be flapping her wings any harder than usual but she had a hundred times the thrust.

'I wonder what fuel these flight boosters run on,' Ruth remarked. 'It seems to be more efficient than poo.'

'There's the fair,' Amy shouted. Part of the park was full of colourful stalls. She adjusted her super-spec headset to chicken-finder mode. 'And that's where the chicken competition's going to be held.' She pointed her wing at a grassy field just beyond the stalls. Some of the chickens were in cages, but most of them, presumably the ones from the coops at Dudley Manor, were pecking about on the grass, fenced in by green wire netting. There were no humans about. They'd all gone off to have breakfast. It was just as Professor Rooster had feared! It was the perfect opportunity for Kebab Claude to strike!

The chickens landed near the hedge. They took off their flight-booster engines and hid them in some brambles. Then they made their way cautiously along the base of the hedge towards the chicken pen.

'Look! There's the worm-burger stand!' Boo pointed to a thicket of bushes a few metres from the far end of the temporary enclosure.

Amy focused her headset. She couldn't see Kebab Claude, but the worm-burger stand looked very sophisticated. A feeding trough hung over the side of a wheelbarrow on big iron hooks. On the other side of the wheelbarrow a pack of burger baps, a bulb of garlic, some olive oil, a tub of wriggling worms and a bottle of barbecue sauce rested upon a fold-out counter. Inside the wheelbarrow was the barbecue. Smoke trickled off the sizzling coals through the grill, which consisted of a piece of old chicken wire. It was just the sort of thing most chickens would love, Amy thought. Honestly, if she didn't know any better, she'd be up there queuing for a worm burger herself!

Just then Kebab Claude stepped out from behind the thicket. As well as his chef's hat, the poodle was wearing a sign round his neck that read 'I'm a chicken'.

As soon as she saw him, Amy relaxed. 'No one's going to fall for that!' she snorted.

Just then there was a commotion inside the chicken pen. 'Look! Worm burgers!' A group of hungry chicks hopped up to the green wire netting and squeezed through it. The gaps in the netting were bigger than the ones in normal chicken wire.

'Except them,' Boo said in a frightened voice.

'Oh no!' Amy gasped. 'We've got to stop them. Ruth, have you got the mite blaster?'

'Check,' Ruth said.

'Okay, follow me.' Amy crept towards the burger stand until she was parallel with the thicket of bushes. 'Pssssst!' she hissed, trying to get the chicks' attention.

The chicks didn't seem to hear her. They were cheeping noisily about what topping they were going to have on their worm burgers.

Kebab Claude had got his spatula out. *NO!* Amy watched in horror as he leaned over the wheelbarrow, flipped the first chick into a bun and threw his hat over the others. He trickled oil over the chick, shoved a clove of garlic in its beak and placed it on the counter. The grill began to sizzle.

'Get ready to fire, Ruth!' Amy whispered.

'Wait! We've got to get the chicks out first!' Ruth said. 'We don't want them to get blasted with mites.'

Amy was glad Ruth was so clever. She hadn't thought about that!

'How?' Boo whispered.

'We need a decoy,' Ruth said.

Amy had an idea. 'I'll keep Kebab occupied,' she said, 'while Boo somersaults over and rescues the chicks. As soon as they're out of the way, Ruth, you blast him.'

'But, Amy . . .' Boo protested. 'It's too dangerous.'

Amy hardly heard her. She scuttled towards the burger stand. 'Hey, hairy chicken dude,' she waved. 'Give me the biggest worm burger you've got. With extra beetle-crunch topping.' She fluffed out her feathers to make herself look plumper.

Kebab Claude looked up. His greedy eyes grew round. He shoved the chick off the counter. The bun bounced on the ground. The chick tumbled out and scurried under the chef's hat with his friends.

''Ow about ze Colossus?' Kebab Claude's eyes were fixed on Amy. He reached under the counter and pulled out an enormous bap.

'I'll take two!' Amy waddled towards the burger stand.

'Sure!' Kebab Claude bent down for another bap.

Out of the corner of her eye, Amy saw Boo somersault forwards and dive under the chef's hat. The hat started to inch slowly away from the burger stand towards Ruth as Boo led the chicks to safety. Amy hopped up on to the counter and pretended to examine the tub of worms. She had to stop

Kebab Claude from noticing the hat was moving!
Quickly she grabbed the bottle of barbecue sauce
and squeezed it hard.

Kebab Claude stood up. *SPLODGE!* A shower of
red goo caught him in the eye.

'I'll get you for zat!' Kebab Claude growled. He
reached for the spatula.

'Amy, get out the way!' Ruth shouted.

Amy flung herself off the counter.

WHOOSH!

A stream of mites hit Kebab Claude in the chest.

'Aaarrgggh!' he howled. He staggered out from behind the wheelbarrow.

WHOOSH!

Ruth blasted him again.

Kebab Claude backed away, snarling.

Ruth raised the mite blaster for the third time.

'Beat it, dog-chops!' Amy cried.

With one last hungry look in her direction, Kebab Claude turned and cantered off towards the Deep Dark Woods.

'He's going!' Amy cried ecstatically. 'We did it!' She flew over to join Boo and Ruth. Ruth dropped the mite blaster on the grass. The three chickens embraced. Just then a tall chicken with smart cream feathers bustled up. 'Chicks!' she cried. 'There you are! I've been looking for you everywhere. I told you not to go outside the wire netting.' Her eye fell upon the worm-burger stand. 'Or eat junk.' Then it fell upon Amy, Boo and Ruth. 'Or talk to strangers.'

'Sorry, Miss Lacey,' the chicks hung their heads.

Amy glanced at Boo and Ruth. Miss Lacey must be the chicks' teacher. She decided not to tell her about Claude Kebab and the rescue mission. She had a feeling it was probably supposed to be a secret anyway. 'Are all the chicks from Dudley Manor?' Amy asked instead.

'Yes,' the teacher nodded proudly. 'We run a little school in the chicken pens. It's called Dudley Coop Academy. We've got about thirty at the moment in the juniors and seniors combined. These are our Month 4s.'

'They're really cute,' Boo said.

The teacher chuckled fondly. 'That's what you think!' she said. 'They're always up to mischief if you don't keep an eye on them.'

'What's this?' one of the chicks asked.

Amy turned round. The chick had picked up the mite blaster.

'Er, put that down please,' said Amy.

'But I want to look at it,' the chick said.

72

'You can't,' Ruth said.

'Can I see it?' another chick asked.

'No,' Amy said.

The chicks paid no attention. They crowded round their friend, pushing and shoving to get a better look at the gadget.

'How does it work?' the first one demanded.

'I'm not going to tell you,' Ruth said.

'Give it to me!' Amy ordered.

'What does this do?' the chick fingered the trigger. He lifted the mite blaster and pointed it at the three chickens.

'No, no, no, no, no!' Amy said.

'You don't want to do that,' Ruth said.

'Really you don't,' Boo pleaded.

'Yes, I do,' the chick insisted. He pulled the trigger.

WHOOSH! A stream of mites accelerated towards Boo, Ruth and Amy.

Uh-oh! Amy thought as the mites hit her in a big black cloud. *The professor's not going to be too happy about this.*

Chapter Seven

At his top-secret location somewhere on the Dudley Estate, Professor Emeritus Rooster went through the eyewitness accounts of the Kebab Claude mission again. The professor scratched his comb. He was trying to piece together how his elite combat squad had ended up with acute mite infestation. And how his precious mite blaster had fallen into the mischievous wings of the Month 4s of Dudley Coop Academy. Professor Rooster sighed. His elite combat squad was good, but it wasn't good enough, whatever Shigong Egg said. It needed sharpening up. It needed, as he had always thought, a professional poultry protector to lead it. Professor Rooster came to a decision. He tapped a few keys on his laptop and spoke into the microphone.

'This is Professor Rooster,' he said. 'Is that Poultry Patrol?'

'Yes,' a voice came back. 'Can I help?'

'I'm looking for a professional poultry protector,' Professor Rooster said. 'A bird who can lead a team.'

'All our bird agents are highly experienced professionals,' the voice came back. 'They won't let you down.'

'Good,' Professor Rooster said. 'Send me the best agent you've got. As soon as possible.'

'What are we going to tell the professor?' Boo asked.

The three chickens lay on their beds at Chicken HQ swathed in cotton wool soaked with anti-itch cream. They made a sorry picture. The cream was oily. It dripped off their feathers on to the hay. Amy felt as if she'd just been seasoned by Kebab Claude and stuck in a cotton-wool burger bap.

'How about we say the mite blaster went off by accident?' Amy suggested. 'He won't know.'

'I'm not sure if he'll believe us,' Ruth said doubtfully. 'I mean, it was working fine before.'

'Do you think he's got an antidote for mite infestation?' Boo moaned. 'My boots itch.'

'Why don't you ask him?' Amy said. 'Look, he's on the computer.'

The screen fizzled. Professor Rooster's stern face appeared.

The chickens struggled out of bed and hobbled over to the cardboard box.

Professor Rooster glared at them. He didn't speak.

Amy coughed. 'Er . . . about the mite blaster, Professor Rooster,' she began.

'Before you say anything,' Professor Rooster interrupted, 'I have read a number of eyewitness accounts of the Kebab mission. So don't think about telling any fibs.'

Amy stared at her toes. She didn't dare look at Boo and Ruth. She wished she hadn't suggested telling the professor that the mite blaster went off by accident. She should have known he would already have investigated what had happened.

'I admit you showed courage, intelligence and perseverance when you rescued the chicks from Kebab Claude's clutches,' the professor continued in a softer voice. 'But it should never have got to that stage: one

of them was only seconds away from getting fried.'
He paused. 'And as for letting the Month 4s pick up
the mite blaster, that was just plain dumb.'

'Sorry,' Amy said.

'That was my fault,' Ruth admitted. 'I dropped it.'

'We wanted a hug,' Boo explained.

'A *hug* . . .' Professor Rooster let the word hang
in the air. 'That's all very sweet but a hug is not
going to defeat our enemies. What if Tiddles had
been there? Or Fox? They would have eaten you
before you could say boiled egg.' He shook his head.
'You may have squeaked through against Kebab
Claude, but you're definitely not ready for Fox.
Which is why I've employed a fourth member of the
squad,' the professor concluded, 'to keep an eye on
you and make sure there are no more cluck-ups.' He
assumed his stern expression. 'Thaddeus E. Fox and
his gang may strike again at any time. They want
chicken and they'll do anything to get it. I need a
team I can rely on. Your new team leader will be
with you shortly. Make sure you do as he tells you.
He's a professional: one of the best. He comes with

the highest recommendations. He'll give you some action points to work on.'

The screen fizzled. Professor Rooster disappeared.

The first potting-shed door flew open.

The chickens twisted awkwardly on their stools to get a look at the newcomer.

The fourth member of the squad strolled in. He was a large mallard duck wearing a crisp bow tie. 'My name's Pond, James Pond,' he said. 'I'm from Poultry Patrol. I gather you hens need some help.'

Amy stared at him, speechless. *I gather you hens need some help?!* Who did he think he was? They didn't need help. Well, maybe just a little bit. But not from some stuck-up duck like James Pond. 'What's Poultry Patrol anyway?' she asked defensively.

'It's a secret organisation dedicated to the protection of poultry,' James Pond told her. 'It accepts only the best birds as agents: the ones with razor-sharp brains, fabulous fighting skills, and super-smooth feathers suitable for long-distance swimming and flying. Like me,' he added.

'Yeah, we get it,' Amy said rudely. James Pond was the worst show-off she'd ever met. She felt like she had to retaliate. '*We* trained at the International School of Kung Fu for Poultry, in case you didn't know,' she boasted.

'I did know,' James Pond responded sharply. 'It's my business to know everything. I also know that *you* can't do Kung Fu because your legs are too short; that Ruth makes rotten-egg stink bombs out of cardboard tubes and fart gas, and that Boo is good at gymnastics but a scaredy-hen when it comes to fighting.'

79

'How do you know all that?' Amy gasped.

'I've read the file. Like I say: you hens need help. That's why the prof hired me: so that *you* do what *I* tell you. That way we might stand a chance against the bad guys. Get it?'

The chickens said nothing. Boo shuffled her feet. Ruth made a little humming noise. Amy puffed out her tummy feathers. It was all she could do to stop herself performing the feather dusty on their new team leader.

'Good,' James Pond said. He looked them up and down. 'Apart from Boo, you hens are pretty out of shape. It's time for some exercise. Let's do some press-ups.'

Amy dropped to her knees and started to push herself wearily up and down. She was rubbish at press-ups, especially when she was all itchy. Not as bad as Ruth though. Poor Ruth had already collapsed. It was only Boo who was any good at doing them from her gymnastics training.

'Well done, Boo,' James Pond said. 'In fact it was *so* good you can do twenty more. You two, that was rubbish. Try sit-ups instead.'

Amy rolled on her back and tried to sit up. She couldn't. Her tummy was too fat. She collapsed backwards on to the floor.

'Pathetic,' James Pond said. 'Right. Let's do some running. Fifty laps of the garden. NOW!'

'I knew I wasn't cut out for this,' Boo puffed as the chickens toiled round the garden path.

'Me neither,' Ruth panted.

'Don't worry,' Amy wheezed. 'We'll show Pond what we're made of. The professor will soon realise we don't need a team leader. Just you wait and see.'

Chapter Eight

Down in a burrow in the Deep Dark Woods, Thaddeus E. Fox drew back his chair and stood up. It was time to address the meeting.

He banged his silver cane on the table.

'Friends,' he said. 'Welcome to this session of the MOST WANTED Club.' He surveyed the group with some irritation. Everyone was present. Tiny Tony Tiddles was there, relaxing in an armchair, looking like he owned the joint. The Pigeon-Poo Gang had made themselves comfortable beside the larder in case any food fell out. And Kebab Claude lay stretched out on the earth floor, whining. Thaddeus E. Fox eyed the poodle with distaste. Kebab Claude was wrapped in oily bandages. Every now and then he raised a hind leg and scratched frantically. Thaddeus E. Fox waited while they all took their places.

'There are three items on the agenda today.' Thaddeus E. Fox handed round some bits of paper.

AGENDA

1. Catching chicken
2. Catching more Chicken
3. Defeating our enemies

He waited patiently while everyone read them. 'Let's start with item three.' He cleared his throat. 'Claude, describe what happened at the country fair again. I want every last detail.'

Kebab Claude sat up painfully. He went through the events leading up to his infestation. 'And zat was when zey blasted me wiz ze mites,' he finished.

'What did they look like?' Thaddeus demanded. 'The chickens that attacked you?'

'One was small and fat with red cheeks,' Claude growled. 'Ze one wiz ze mite blaster had glasses. Zey were both young. I didn't see no ozzers.'

'But we can assume, I think, that there was a third bird,' Thaddeus E. Fox deduced, 'who assisted the chicks to safety. Think, Kebab, did you see the hat move?'

'Now you come to mention it, I think I did!' Kebab scratched his ear.

'So, what we have is a team of three chickens equipped with a powerful mite blaster turning up in the nick of time to rescue of a bunch of school chicks,' Thaddeus E. Fox mused. His yellow eyes narrowed. 'It's got Rooster written all over it.'

'What, that professor dude?' Tony Tiddles demanded. 'The one that kept crowing to alert the humans? I thought you finished him off.'

'Unfortunately not, my friend,' Thaddeus E. Fox said. 'Only his family. He escaped. I think this is his idea of revenge.' Suddenly he started to laugh. 'Phwa ha ha ha ha! Three kid chickens against the villainous talents of the MOST WANTED Club?! Rooster hasn't got a prayer!'

The other members of the Club laughed too, except the Pigeon-Poo Gang, who cooed instead.

Thaddeus E. Fox banged his cane on the table. 'Let us return to the agenda. Items one and two, to be precise. But we shall have to be vigilant. We shall have to outsmart Rooster and his chicken squad.'

He licked his chops. 'Anyone got any ideas?'

Tony Tiddles put his paw up slowly. 'I've got an idea,' he said. 'But I might need some aerial support if those chickens show up again.'

Thaddeus E. Fox raised an eyebrow in the direction of the Pigeon-Poo Gang. They huddled together. 'Okay,' their leader agreed. 'We'll do what we can. We've already got mites anyway.'

'And fleas,' another member of the gang added.

'And worms,' said the third.

Thaddeus E. Fox took a step away from them. 'Er . . . okay, Tony, what's the plan?'

'Well, it's not chickens exactly,' Tony said. 'It's waterfowl.'

'Waterfowl?' Thaddeus E. Fox repeated.

'Yeah, you know: ducks, geese, swans,' Tiny Tony explained.

'I know what waterfowl are, Tiddles,' Thaddeus E. Fox said impatiently. 'I also know that they spend a lot of time swimming and that I don't particularly like getting wet unless it's a very warm day. So what's the plan?'

'I was up at Dudley Manor this morning snooping around,' Tiny Tony said, 'and I noticed the humans have built a new birdhouse on the island for the waterfowl. There's tons of them there.'

'But how do we reach them?' Thaddeus E. Fox demanded.

'That's the beauty of it,' Tiny Tony grinned. 'We don't have to go to the island at all. The humans are so dumb they put food down for the birds on the grass bank opposite, so the birds swim over to feed.

Then they get drowsy and have a little sleep. All we need to do is sneak up on them and *bam*!' He told the MOST WANTED villains his plan.

Thaddeus E. Fox nodded approvingly. 'Very nice, Tony. Very nice.' He licked his lips. 'I'll take my goose with extra apple sauce.'

'Up you get!'

Amy felt a large webbed foot plant itself on her backside. It was Pond's. 'Go away,' she groaned. 'It's Sunday. I want a lie-in.' Her parents had always let her have a lie-in at Perrin's Farm on a Sunday.

'Now!' Pond shouted. 'Or I'll kick your butt.'

'Okay, I'm coming!' Amy croaked. Pond had kicked her butt the day before and it was still bruised.

'Outside!' Pond quacked.

'But I haven't had any breakfast!' Amy protested.

'Too bad.'

Amy stumbled out of the door into the vegetable garden.

'Put your flight–booster engine on,' Pond ordered.

'Here you are, Amy.' Ruth held it out to her. She and Boo were already wearing theirs.

'Where are we going?' Amy yawned.

'On a mission,' Boo whispered. 'Professor Rooster was on the computer this morning. Only Pond won't tell us what it is he wants us to do.'

'Pond's so annoying!' Amy stormed. 'It's like he wants to get all the credit.'

'Stop squawking and follow me,' Pond thundered.

James Pond lolloped along the garden path, flapping his wings furiously. Amy was pleased to see he didn't look much better at taking off than she was. Once he was in the air though, Amy had to admit, Pond was a good flyer. His wing strokes were powerful and his long neck stretched out in front of him like a missile seeking its target. He zoomed over the garden wall and out over the park. Amy had to put her flight booster on MAX to keep up with him.

Chicken HQ was at the northern end of the park. Amy could see the great stone bulk of Dudley

Manor ahead of them. To the left of the house was where the chickens lived in their coops, penned in with wire. Amy assumed that was their destination: Fox and his cronies must be mounting an attack on the pens! She hoped they'd be in time. To her surprise, however, James Pond flew in the opposite direction – west, towards the river.

Amy flapped alongside him. 'Where are we going?' she puffed. 'The chicken runs are the other way.'

'It's not the chickens we're concerned about,' Pond quacked. 'Professor Rooster got a tip-off from his spies in the Deep Dark Woods. Tiny Tony Tiddles has teamed up with the Pigeon-Poo Gang. They're going after the waterfowl. Tiddles and the rest of the MOST WANTED Club get the birds. The Pigeon-Poo Gang scoff the birdseed. Easy pickings.' He grunted. 'Except they hadn't planned on James Pond being around.'

'Or us,' Amy muttered defiantly. She fell back in line with Boo and Ruth, giving them a wave of encouragement. They smiled back weakly. Amy

knew they were just as fed up with James Pond as she was. Especially Boo, after that mean thing Pond had said about her being a scaredy-hen. If only they could work out a way of getting rid of him! Amy was sure they didn't need his help. They just needed a bit more practice; that was all.

'Coming in to land,' James Pond shouted. He flew low over the river, raising his head and chest up and slowing the beat of his wings, landing elegantly with the tiniest of splashes in the water. He swam over to the rushes on the edge of the grassy bank.

Amy landed with a bump on the lawn. Boo and Ruth dropped down next to her.

James Pond waddled up. He had a net bag of peanuts in his beak, which he laid at the chickens' feet. 'Go upriver, keeping out of sight,' he ordered. 'When you're opposite the island throw some peanuts on to the grass. The Pigeon-Poo Gang will be there like a shot. They can't resist muscling in on someone else's lunch. It's in their DNA. You keep them busy; I'll deal with Tiddles. Watch out though – make sure you hide the rest of the nuts or the pigeons will be after you.'

Amy picked up the bag of peanuts and tucked it under her wing. 'It's not fair, she said. 'He gets to have all the fun.'

Chapter Nine

The chickens clambered along the bank through the rushes. It was hard work, Amy thought, unless you had great big webbed feet, like Pond. Her toes kept getting sucked into the mud.

'My boots are getting filthy,' Boo sniffed.

'Never mind,' Amy consoled her. 'You can have a nice bath when you get back and clean them with some Bird Bright.'

'I can't!' Boo said sadly. 'Pond's used it all.'

'Honestly!' said Amy. 'That duck's a right pain in the bum!'

'And he's locked the gadget cupboard so I can't get in it,' Ruth lamented. 'He won't even let me invent anything in case I get it wrong. He says hens can't do things like that.'

'For goodness' sake!' said Amy. She was getting crosser and crosser with James Pond. Of course Ruth could invent things! She was brilliant at it.

And Boo wasn't a scaredy-hen. She was brave. She deserved her Bird Bright baths. Pond just had to stick his beak into everything. In the week since he'd arrived he'd even nabbed the computer for himself. He wouldn't let Amy watch the wrestling. He just wanted to watch holiday programmes so he could boast about all the places he'd been to in the world. Amy stomped along, fuming.

Ruth interrupted her musings. 'Maybe if we do a good job today,' Ruth was saying in her practical voice, 'we could ask Professor Rooster nicely if we can do the next mission on our own.'

'That's a good idea,' Boo agreed.

'But we're hardly doing *anything*,' Amy grumbled. 'Professor Rooster won't be impressed. Pond's doing all the rescuing; all we have to do is throw a bunch of peanuts at some pigeons.' She puffed out her cheeks and blew a big, fed-up sigh.

'Maybe it'll be more exciting than you think,' Boo said. 'I mean, Professor Rooster did say that the pigeons were dangerous.'

'I doubt it,' Amy muttered.

Ruth was in front of them. She stopped suddenly. 'There's the island!' she said.

Amy peered out from the rushes. A big white birdhouse with a red roof and ivy growing up the walls stood on a small island in the middle of the river.

'Where are the waterfowl?' Boo whispered, creeping up beside her.

'I don't know,' Amy replied. The birdhouse was empty.

'Over here,' Ruth hissed. 'On the bank.'

Amy squeezed her way back through the rushes. The waterfowl had swum across the river from the birdhouse to feed. They were sunning themselves on the lawn that stretched down to the river from the manor house.

'Oh no,' said Amy. 'They're sitting ducks! We need to get them back across to the island before Tiddles strikes.'

'Too late,' Boo said. She pointed up the lawn.

Tiny Tony Tiddles was crawling along the grass towards the snoozing waterfowl.

Amy waved frantically at the sleepy birds. 'Watch

out!' she squawked. 'There's a cat.'

Some of the waterfowl woke up. They scrambled to their feet.

'Retreat to the river!' shouted Ruth. 'Go back to the birdhouse. Mayday! Mayday!'

More of the waterfowl woke up. They flocked this way and that in a panic.

Just then there was a rustle of wings.

'The Pigeon-Poo Gang!' Boo screeched.

Amy watched aghast as three grey and purple birds in shades appeared out of a tree and circled the garden.

'Quick, Amy! Throw the peanuts,' Ruth urged.

Amy scuttled out of the rushes and threw some peanuts on the grass. She scurried back to her friends, being careful to hide the peanut net under her wing so as not to draw attention to their presence.

The Pigeon-Poo Gang swooped on to the lawn. Within seconds they'd scoffed all the nuts plus all the feed the waterfowl had missed.

'It's not going to stop them!' Amy cried. The Pigeon-Poo Gang had already taken off again.

'They're heading for the water,' Ruth reported. 'I think they're going to launch an aerial bombardment.'

The Pigeon-Poo Gang flew low over the river, turned around and zoomed back towards the waterfowl.

PHUT!PHUT!PHUT!PHUT!PHUT!PHUT!

They let out a volley of droppings.

The waterfowl stumbled about, not knowing which way to go. They were sandwiched between Tiny Tony Tiddles on one side and the Pigeon-Poo Gang on the other.

'It's a trap!' Amy shrieked. 'Where's Pond? He's supposed to be here by now.'

SPLASH!SPLASH!SPLASH!SPLASH!SPLASH!

Just then she heard a noise. It was coming from the other side of the rushes.

'Look!' said Ruth.

Amy stared in amazement. James Pond was approaching the bank, his neck outstretched and his webbed feet splashing madly; whirring round like paddles on a demented pedalo.

 96

'Duck!' Pond shouted.

The chickens ducked.

James Pond shot out of the river and into the air. He whizzed over the rushes and past the terrified waterfowl, ramrod straight, without opening his wings.

BOING!!!!

He whammed straight into Tiny Tony Tiddles, knocking him out with his beak.

'You've got to admit, that duck's got class,' Ruth said reluctantly.

PHUT!PHUT!PHUT!PHUT!PHUT!PHUT!

The Pigeon-Poo Gang commenced another attack.

'Quick, Amy,' Boo said. 'They haven't given up yet. They're going after Pond.'

'Throw the peanuts!' Ruth yelled.

'Okay, come and get it!' Amy scuttled out of the rushes and scattered some more peanuts on the grass. She was about to empty them all out when her stomach gave a growl. Amy remembered she hadn't had any breakfast. She hesitated. There were tons of peanuts on the lawn. It would keep the pigeons busy for a bit. Long enough for her, Boo and Ruth to have a quick snack without the pigeons noticing. She counted seven nuts: three for her and two each for Boo and Ruth.

'Hurry up!' Boo cried.

'Coming!' Amy hurried back to her hiding place. 'Here,' she handed her friends a peanut.

PHUT!PHUT!PHUT!PHUT!PHUT!PHUT!

A hail of droppings landed on the chickens.

'Aaarrggghh!' Boo screamed. 'It's the Pigeon-Poo Gang! They're after our nuts!'

Amy could hardly believe it. They must have finished the peanuts on the grass already! She'd never imagined any bird could eat so quickly. Suddenly she remembered what Professor Rooster had said about the Pigeon-Poo Gang: *Don't be fooled. These are some of the greediest, grottiest gangsters I've ever come across on the Dudley Estate.* Amy gulped. She shouldn't have underestimated the pigeons. And she'd put Boo and Ruth in danger. They were about to get sludged.

'Hide the peanuts, Amy!' Boo shrieked, diving for cover.

PHUT!PHUT!PHUT!PHUT!PHUT!PHUT!

'I can't see them!' Amy screamed. She had pigeon poo in her eyes.

'Quick, Amy!' Ruth yelled. 'Before they sludge us to death!'

'It's too late!' Boo sobbed. 'The pigeons have landed.'

The three pigeons fluttered about in the rushes,

scratching and pecking at the chickens, desperate for more nuts.

'Do something, someone!' Boo screeched.

'I can't move!' Ruth lay on her back in the mud. 'That poo's stronger than superglue! I'm stuck in the mud!'

'My eyelids are glued together!' Amy squawked.

'My beautiful boots!' Boo wept. 'I'll have to have them plucked!'

'*HISSSSSSSSSS! SSSSSSSSSSSSSS!*'

'What's going on?' Amy looked about blindly. She heard the squelch of feet. Then honking. And quacking. And more hissing. The cacophony of noises rose all around her in a great din.

'It's Pond,' Ruth's voice rose over the sound. 'He's attacking the pigeons. The rest of the waterfowl are helping him.'

'*HISSSSSSS! QUACK! HONK!*' The battle continued.

Finally Amy heard the rustle of feathers and a last desperate 'coo'.

'The pigeons have gone!' Boo told her.

'Phew!' Amy said. 'Thank goodness that's over.'

Just then something grabbed her by the scruff of her neck. She felt herself being lifted in the air. The next thing she knew she was being plunged into freezing-cold water. Something rubbed at her eyes. Amy struggled and flapped. But whatever it was kept rubbing, pausing occasionally to let her up for air.

Eventually she landed back on the bank.

She opened her eyes. They weren't glued together any more. James Pond was standing over her. She glanced to the side. Boo and Ruth were lying nearby, their legs in the air, gasping for breath. They were both bedraggled, like her, but clean. At least, Amy thought, trying to look on the bright side, Boo's boots hadn't been plucked.

'Thanks for helping the hens,' Pond nodded to the other waterfowl.

Amy realised she must have been dunked by one of the ducks or geese. It was their rough feathers she had felt rubbing the gunk out of her eyes.

'Now go home,' Pond said. 'The show's over.'

 101

The waterfowl swam back to the little house on the island, honking and quacking.

Boo gave a deep sigh. 'I *really* don't think I'm cut out for this,' she said in a weak voice.

'Me neither,' Ruth croaked.

Amy said nothing. As long as Pond was on the scene, she wasn't sure she'd ever be able to squawk them round.

Chapter Ten

Down in a burrow in the Deep Dark Woods, Thaddeus E. Fox drew back his chair and stood up. It was time to address the meeting.

He banged his silver cane on the table.

'Friends,' he said. 'Welcome to this emergency session of the MOST WANTED Club.' He surveyed the group. Tiny Tony Tiddles was clutching an ice pack to his head. Kebab Claude kept looking nervously about as if he was being followed. So did the Pigeon-Poo Gang. Thaddeus E. Fox narrowed his cunning yellow eyes. His fellow villains were spooked. It was time to take charge of the situation before they panicked completely.

'There are three items on the agenda again today.' Thaddeus E. Fox handed round some bits of paper.

AGENDA

1. Catching chicken
2. Catching more chicken
3. ~~De~~feating our enemies

He waited patiently while everyone read it. 'Let's start with item three.' He cleared his throat. 'Tiny Tony: describe exactly what happened last Sunday. I want every last detail.'

Tiny Tony Tiddles went through the events leading up to when he received his knockout blow.

'I'm assuming the chickens were the same as the ones at the Dudley Manor Country Fair,' Thaddeus E. Fox remarked. 'Only this time, they had help.' He threw down a drawing of James Pond. 'Is this the duck?'

'That's him all right,' Tony Tiddles snarled. 'What I wanna know is what you're gonna do about it, Fox, seeing as it's your fault Rooster hired these guys in the first place.'

Thaddeus E. Fox eyed Tiny Tony with dislike. He

didn't like being challenged by a fellow villain. He felt tempted to bash the cat over the head with his silver cane, use his whiskers to make a nailbrush and ask Kebab Claude to barbecue him. But Tiny Tony had the respect of the other members of the MOST WANTED Club. He would have to be careful.

'I'm going to get rid of him,' Thaddeus E. Fox said blandly. He cleared his throat. 'However, as I'm sure you're aware, the first rule of warfare is to know your enemies. Ours are Rooster, the duck and the three chickens.' He placed pictures of Boo, Ruth and Amy on to the table beside Pond's. 'It has come to my knowledge that Rooster's intention was to create an elite team of chicken warriors under the tutelage of the great Shigong Egg,' Thaddeus E. Fox explained. 'They trained at the International School of Kung Fu for Poultry in Tibet.' His face twisted into a malicious grin. 'Nice idea,' he smirked, 'except it didn't work.'

'That's easy for you to say!' Kebab Claude growled. 'You didn't get blasted with mites.' He was still itching.

Thaddeus E. Fox didn't reply directly. 'Look at what happened after they whacked you with that mite blaster.' He placed two photographs on the table. 'The weasels took them,' he explained.

The first was a close-up of the Month 4 chicks holding the mite blaster; the second of Boo, Ruth and Amy smothered in mite bites. 'They got blasted by a four-month-old chick, who they were supposed to be rescuing.'

'Serves zem right,' Kebab Claude growled.

'My guess is that's why Rooster hired the duck: to help his chicken squad out of a hole,' Thaddeus E. Fox went on. 'The duck's name is Pond: James Pond. He's from Poultry Patrol. It's him we need to watch out for. Without him the chickens are no threat to us' – he doffed his top hat towards the Pigeon-Poo

Gang – 'as our friends proved on Sunday. Good work, boys.'

'Thank coo,' the Pigeon-Poo Gang bobbed their heads in acknowledgement.

Thaddeus E. Fox smoothed his whiskers. 'Rooster thinks he can outsmart us,' he said. 'But without Pond, he's got nothing.'

'Brilliant, Sherlock!' Tiny Tony spat sarcastically. 'But like I said, the question is what are you gonna to do about it?'

'I'll fix Pond,' Thaddeus E. Fox said quietly.

'How?' Tiddles snorted. 'Seems like he's got all the aces up those wings of his.'

'I said I'll fix him,' Thaddeus E. Fox hissed. It was time to show the MOST WANTED Club who was boss. 'And if you don't believe me, I'll fix you too.'

Tony Tiddles fell silent.

'And ze chickens?' Kebab Claude demanded.

Thaddeus E. Fox laughed. 'Chickens?' he sneered. 'Have you seen what I do to chickens? Those three jokers wouldn't last ten seconds with me. Not even five if I'm in a bad mood. I might pluck them before

I eat them just to make it more fun. Or pull their entrails out and make sausages with them.'

'Or kebabs,' Kebab Claude suggested.

'Indeed!' Thaddeus swept the pictures of Pond and the chickens into the bin. 'Consider it done, gentlemen. Our enemies will be eliminated. You have my word.' He paused. 'And once they're out of the way, we shall return to items one and two on the agenda.' He threw back his head and laughed. 'Phwa ha ha ha ha. I believe, gentlemen, it is *my* turn to hatch an evil plan. And this time I guarantee it will not fail. Now, can anyone tell me where to find the Bird Broadcasting Company?'

Chapter Eleven

The next morning Amy was woken up by the sound of the computer. She listened closely. It wasn't Professor Rooster who was speaking, it was a low growly voice she didn't recognise. Amy groaned. It was probably one of James Pond's rotten holiday programmes. She closed her eyes, snuggled down in the straw bed beside Boo and Ruth and tried to go back to sleep.

A few minutes later she heard a loud bang. It sounded like the door of the potting shed swinging closed. Her first thought was panic: *what if the MOST WANTED villains had discovered their hideout? What if Fox had come to kill them?* She waited, her heart pounding. Nothing happened. After a few minutes she decided to investigate. Boo and Ruth were still sleeping. Amy wriggled quietly out of bed and slid off the straw so as not to disturb them. She looked around the potting shed. There was no sign of Pond.

James Pond normally slept in a pile of leaves next to the gadget cupboard, but he wasn't there. And he wasn't beside the computer either, even though the TV channel was still playing. Where had he gone? Amy swallowed. *Had Thaddeus E. Fox and his cronies eaten him?* There was no trace of any feathers. James Pond had simply vanished.

Cautiously she tiptoed to the potting-shed door and pushed it open. She was almost relieved to see James Pond standing outside on the garden path doing some limbering up exercises. He looked as if he was preparing to take off.

'What are you doing?' Amy asked. 'Is there another mission?'

'No,' James Pond said. 'I'm leaving.'

'Leaving?' Amy squawked. It was too good to be true. 'Why? Did the professor fire you?'

'No,' James Pond snapped. 'I'm migrating south for the winter. The Caribbean probably.' He flapped his wings energetically.

'But it's the summer!' Amy felt confused. She squinted at the blue sky. The sun was shining. It was

a beautiful day. 'It's months until winter. We've got autumn still to go.'

'I just checked the weather forecast on the BBC,' Pond quacked. 'Winter's coming early this year. Blizzards by Thursday, that's what it said.'

'Are you sure?' Amy said doubtfully. 'It's only July.'

'Of course, I'm sure,' Pond said. 'The BBC's always right with the weather forecast.'

'Have you told Professor Rooster?' Amy asked.

'No, I don't have time. I need to start flying. You tell him.' James Pond did a few knee bends. 'He can always get another agent from Poultry Patrol to help out you hens, if that's what you're worried about.'

Amy didn't reply. She hardly heard him. She was thinking about the weather forecast. Something weird was going on.

'See you around.' James Pond started his lopsided run, his wings beating up and down. Very soon he was in the air. Amy watched him as he disappeared over the garden wall, then she ran back into the potting sheds.

'Boo! Ruth! Wake up!'

Boo and Ruth emerged yawning from the straw.

'What's the matter?' Ruth asked.

'Is it Professor Rooster?' Boo said, stretching. 'Has he got another mission for us?'

'No,' Amy flapped. 'It's Pond. He's gone!'

Boo and Ruth looked at her in astonishment. 'Gone?' they chorused.

'He thinks it's going to snow!' Amy quickly repeated what Pond had told her about the weather forecast. 'He's migrating south for the winter.'

'But it's only July!' Boo said.

'That's exactly what I said,' Amy told her. 'He said he'd seen it on the BBC.'

Ruth's glasses wiggled. 'Blizzards in summer? That can't be right. Not in the northern hemisphere anyway. Let's check the forecast.'

The chickens hurried over to the computer. The BBC weather forecast was still showing on the screen. A giant chicken stood in front of a world map, holding a silver-tipped cane. 'As I was saying,' it growled, 'winter is coming early this year thanks

to this cold front from Siberia.' It used the cane to point to a swirly mass of cloud edging towards the UK. 'There will definitely be blizzards by Thursday and they won't be going anywhere until at least April next year.' The giant chicken looked straight at the camera. 'So, if you're a duck, and you haven't left already, I recommend you head south immediately. I repeat, IMMEDIATELY.' Its yellow eyes glinted. 'The Caribbean is particularly pleasant at this time of year.'

'There's something funny about that chicken,' Amy said. 'Did you see its eyes?'

'And its teeth?' Boo shuddered.

Ruth adjusted her glasses. 'It's not a chicken,' she said shortly. 'Look.'

Amy watched breathlessly as Ruth tapped away on some keys. The pictures of the MOST WANTED Club scrolled across the screen.

'There.'

Amy found herself staring at the pictures of Thaddeus E. Fox, the only one of Professor Rooster's cast of villains they hadn't encountered yet. Thaddeus E. Fox in top hat and tails carrying a decapitated chicken. Thaddeus E. Fox by a pond full of dead ducks. Thaddeus E. Fox at a posh picnic.

'See?' Ruth said. 'The cane: it's in all of them.'

Amy drew in her breath sharply. Ruth was right. In every single one of the pictures the MOST WANTED criminal of all was clutching a silver-topped cane.

'And the teeth,' Amy whispered, 'they're definitely his.'

'And the eyes,' Boo shivered.

'Tiny Tony Tiddles must have tipped him off about Pond,' Ruth said. 'And he worked out a way to get rid of him without risking his own foxy fur by pretending to be a BBC weather forecaster and telling Pond winter was coming early. That can only mean one thing . . .' Her voice trailed off.

'He's planning another chicken raid on the coops,' Amy whispered.

There was silence for moment.

'So what shall we do?' Boo asked eventually. 'I mean, with Pond gone, I guess it's up to us now.'

The chickens glanced at one another.

'I'm in,' said Amy.

'Me too,' Ruth said.

'Boo?' Amy waited. 'Will you do it? You're not a scaredy-hen by the way: Pond's an idiot.'

'Okay,' Boo agreed. 'I'll try.'

Amy couldn't help grinning. She knew her friends wouldn't let her down. Then her face became serious. It was too late to send for another agent from Poultry Patrol. Professor Rooster would have

to trust them. And this was their chance to prove to him that he could. 'Let's contact Professor Rooster,' she said in a determined voice. 'Now!'

Chapter Twelve

Thaddeus E. Fox stepped out of his chicken suit. He picked up his cane, collected his top hat and waistcoat and made his way towards the door of the Bird Broadcasting Corporation building.

The BBC headquarters was in a disused barn on an organic farm about ten miles away from the Dudley Estate. It had been easy enough to find. The Pigeon-Poo Gang had forced the information out of other birds in the Deep Dark Woods by threatening to sludge them to death.

'You can release the prisoners now,' Thaddeus E. Fox said.

The Pigeon-Poo Gang hopped out of the shadows. They opened the hayloft. Terrified birds of different varieties tumbled out.

'Do you want to kill them, Boss?' The leader of the pigeons asked.

Thaddeus E. Fox shook his head. 'No.' Part of the

fun of being the most evil villain known to poultry was to keep your enemies guessing. That way, you stayed one paw ahead of them. Professor Rooster would soon find out that Pond had disappeared, if he didn't know already. And that it was he, Thaddeus E. Fox, who had tricked the brilliant duck agent. Rooster would be expecting blood on the straw of the BBC after what had happened to his family. And what happened to his family served Rooster right for crowing to the humans in the first place.

Thaddeus E. Fox smiled. Rooster would be in for a surprise when he discovered all the BBC workers were safe and well. And that would make him nervous. He would know that Thaddeus E. Fox had something TRULY HORRIBLE in mind.

'Leave the prisoners tied up,' he snarled. 'Let's go.' No doubt the rest of the Professor's so-called elite combat squad would be on their way soon. Thaddeus E. Fox sneered at the thought. Let the chickens come. He couldn't care less about them. He had other plans.

The Pigeon-Poo Gang shuffled out of the barn doors and flew away.

Thaddeus E. Fox made his way stealthily across the field. Then he sped back across country to the Dudley Estate.

Tony Tiddles met him at the edge of the Deep Dark Woods.

'Pond's on his way to the Caribbean,' Tiddles reported. 'We saw him flying over Dudley Manor, heading south. My guess is he won't be coming back till spring.'

'Excellent.' Thaddeus E. Fox smiled. 'Let's get back to the burrow. It's time to return to items one and two on the agenda.'

The other villains were waiting for them.

'I'll be with you in a moment.' Thaddeus E. Fox went to the larder. It was hungry work running twenty miles across country. He was beginning to regret his generosity towards the BBC workers. He should have eaten a few when he had the chance. Consoling himself with the thought of some nice juicy chicken, he helped himself to half a dozen

dried mice and an apple and gulped them down hungrily. Then he returned to the table, unrolled a map and placed stones on the corners.

The villains pored over it.

'Observe.' Thaddeus E. Fox pointed with his cane.

'Over here are the Dudley Manor chicken pens.' He

traced a path with the cane across the map to a different spot. 'And over here, on the edge of the Deep Dark Woods, is Eat'em College for Gentlemen Foxes: the greatest school in Britain.' He placed the cane on the table and folded his arms.

The villains waited.

'You won't be surprised to learn that Eat'em College is my old school,' Thaddeus E. Fox boasted. 'It taught me everything I know. Latin, Greek, a love of poetry, how to dress like a gentleman, how to boss other villains around, how to play Foxington Football . . .' He sighed. 'Good times.'

'Why don't you just get to the point?' Tiny Tony Tiddles grumbled.

'I'm about to,' Thaddeus E. Fox gave him a cold look. 'And it's this. Every year on the last Saturday in July, one of the college's old boys organises an Eat'em reunion dinner.'

'That's tomorrow,' Kebab Claude exclaimed.

'Quite,' Thaddeus E. Fox continued. 'This year it's my turn, and I thought we could invite our friends, the pupils of Dudley Coop Academy and

their dear parents and hard-working teachers to join us for the evening.' His eyes gleamed.

'Zey'll never come!' Kebab Claude protested.

'Oh yes, they will,' Thaddeus E. Fox said. 'They're chickens. They're stupid, apart from Rooster. They're trusting. They're dumb. They're greedy. And I have the perfect plan to lure them there. All we have to do

is make a hole in the humans' fortifications and let the chickens do the rest. That way we get the whole lot of them: enough to feed us all. I promise you, they won't suspect a thing.'

'What about Rooster?' Tiny Tony Tiddles demanded. 'Won't he tip them off?'

'All his spies here in the Deep Dark Woods have had their beaks glued,' Thaddeus E. Fox said, 'by our pigeon friends. By the time he finds out his flock's flown the coop, it'll be too late.'

'And the chicken squad?' Tiny Tony still wasn't satisfied.

Thaddeus E. Fox licked his lips. 'Even if his chicken squad shows up, there's only one place for it. And that's on the menu with the rest of them. We'll pluck them, roast them and serve them up with lumpy custard – another wonderful Eat'em College tradition! Now, who's with me?'

'Me,' Kebab Clauded nodded. 'Except for ze lumpy custard.'

'Sure,' Tiny Tony relaxed. 'I take my chicken southern fried with sweetcorn and mayonnaise.'

123

'What's in it for us?' The leader of the Pigeon-Poo Gang asked.

'There's semolina for pudding,' Thaddeus E. Fox told him promptly.

'Coo! Coo! Coo!' The pigeons fluttered excitedly.

'That's settled then. Thank you, gentlemen. You can leave the rest to me.' Thaddeus E. Fox closed the meeting and showed the villains to the door of the burrow. 'See you tomorrow evening at the banquet . . .' He laughed. 'Phwa ha ha ha ha . . . for murder most fowl.'

After the others had left, Thaddeus E. Fox returned to the table and sat down. He opened a drawer and took out a piece of expensive headed notepaper. The address on the top was Eat'em College. Thaddeus E. Fox smiled. He found a black pen and some Tipp-Ex. Then very carefully he painted out a word with the Tipp-Ex and began to write. When he was sure the Tipp-Ex and the ink were dry he rolled the piece of paper into a scroll, unscrewed the silver tip of his cane, placed the paper inside it, and replaced the end. Satisfied with his work, he curled up for a quick nap. Then, when it was pitch-dark, he picked up his cane and made his way silently out of the burrow, through the Deep Dark Woods to the wire of the chicken pens and there, very quietly, he started to dig.

Chapter Thirteen

The next morning the hen-mistress of Dudley Coop Academy was sitting at her desk, writing end of term reports, when her secretary came in with a scroll of paper.

'This arrived for you last night,' the secretary said.

'Thank you.' The hen-mistress took the scroll and unrolled it.

Inside was an invitation.

Don't Eat'em College for
Ladies and Gentlemen Chickens

Invites you to
an Open Evening and Fair
Tonight at 6.00 pm

Barbecue!

Semolina!

Games and Prizes!

Bring the family and all your friends!

———————

Don't Eat'em College for
Ladies and Gentlemen Chickens

The Deep Dark Woods
Dudley Estate,
Berkshire

'That sounds fun!' the hen-mistress said. 'I'll pin it up on the door so that all the parents see it when they come to collect the chicks at home time. I'm sure lots and lots of them will want to go.' She frowned. 'If we can get out of the chicken pen, that is.'

'Oh, don't worry about that,' the secretary reassured her. 'Someone dug a hole under the fence last night.'

'Great!' the hen-mistress said. 'That's a big help. I'm sure we'll all have a lovely time.'

Later that morning at Chicken HQ, Amy sat dejectedly on her stool in front of the computer with Boo and Ruth beside her.

'What's Fox up to?' Professor Rooster was back on the screen. 'What??!!' He limped backwards and forwards across the picture.

Amy wished she could tell him. The problem was she didn't know.

'It's something terrible. I can feel it in my feathers.' Professor Rooster sighed. 'I wish Pond was here,' he muttered. 'With him we might have stood a chance. Now . . .' He didn't finish the sentence.

'There's still a chance, Professor,' Amy said quietly. 'We're a good team. Even without Pond.'

'Amy's right, Professor,' Boo said. 'We are. Honestly.'

'Remember what Shigong Egg said?' Ruth chipped in. 'We've got courage, intelligence and perseverance. We can do it. Really, we can.'

'Do what, though? That's the question?' Professor Rooster responded gloomily.

Amy was thinking hard. Ruth's mention of Shigong Egg had reminded her of something. 'What were those nutty things Shigong Egg used to say?' she asked her friends.

'The road to wisdom lies through sheep dung?' Boo suggested.

'No, not that one.' Amy scratched her head.

'It takes many steps to reach the top floor . . . unless you take the lift?' Ruth said.

'No, not that either . . .' Amy closed her eyes. She concentrated hard. 'Wait! I've got it! "Know your enemy",' she said triumphantly. 'That was it. "Know your enemy". That's what we've got to do with Fox.'

'You mean maybe if we can get into Fox's head, we can work out what he's planning?' Ruth said slowly.

'Yes.'

'Good thinking, Amy!' Boo exclaimed.

Some of the chickens' enthusiasm seemed to have rubbed off on Professor Rooster. 'You're right, chickens,' he said. 'We need to know everything about him. Everything. From what he likes for breakfast . . .'

'To what his favourite colour is . . .' Boo said.

'To what books he reads . . .' Ruth suggested

'To where he went to school.' Amy chipped in.

'By god, Amy!' Professor Rooster cried. 'That's it! The college.'

'The college?' Amy repeated.

Professor Rooster nodded. 'Remember I told you that Thaddeus E. Fox was educated at Eat'em College for Gentlemen Foxes?'

The chickens nodded.

'There's a reunion every year for the old boys,' Professor Rooster told them. 'A dinner. Thaddeus and all his old foxy classmates go. It's always held at Eat'em College on the edge of the Deep Dark Woods.'

'When is it?' Ruth demanded.

'The last Saturday in July.'

Amy checked the calendar. 'That's today! We'd better get down to the chicken pens.'

'But he can't get into the pens,' Ruth reminded her. 'The humans strengthened the wire after the last raid, didn't they, Professor? And even if he *could* get in he wouldn't be able to take enough chickens to feed all those foxes.'

Amy screwed her eyes tight shut again. She felt she was on the verge of a flash of chicken inspiration. 'What if he doesn't *want* to get in?' she asked. 'What if he wants *them* to get out?'

'What do you mean, Amy?' Boo asked.

'What if he invited them?' Amy said. 'To the banquet?'

'They wouldn't go,' Ruth said promptly. 'No chicken would accept an invitation to a foxes' banquet.'

'What if they didn't *know* it was a foxes' banquet,' Amy persisted. 'What if they thought it was something else? What if they thought it was something more *chickeny*?'

The others stared at her.

'They'd never fall for it,' Ruth said.

'Yes, they would,' Amy insisted. 'The Month 4 chicks fell for Kebab Claude's worm-burger stand.'

'Amy's right,' Boo whispered. 'They didn't suspect a thing.'

'But what about the grown-up chickens?' Ruth said. 'Surely they'd realise something was up?'

'Not necessarily,' Professor Rooster said heavily. 'That's the problem with the flock. They're too trusting. And they don't know about the foxes' banquet or where Thaddeus E. Fox went to school. It's quite possible Fox *could* dupe them into going there. It's just the sort of sneaky, freaky, despicable, detestable, vile, sordid, wretched, loathsome, lousy, wicked, rotten, inhuman trick that lowlife fox would play to look good in front of his friends.' He fixed the chickens with a stern stare. 'Right, team,' he said. 'You'd better get over to the pens straight away. I just pray you're not too late.'

Despite the danger of the situation, Amy couldn't help feeling a flicker of delight. The professor trusted

them to do the job. Without James Pond! And they wouldn't let him down. 'Don't worry, Professor,' she said in a businesslike tone. 'We'll stop him.'

'Take the Emergency Chicken Pack,' the professor ordered. 'You'll find some things in there that might help you.'

Ruth rummaged about in the gadget cupboard. 'Got it!' She strapped the pack around her neck.

The chickens clipped themselves into their flight boosters and hopped out of the potting sheds.

Chapter Fourteen

A few minutes later the chickens arrived at the pens. To their horror they were empty. The chickens of Dudley Manor had disappeared.

'They must have got out under here,' Ruth scratched at the hole under the fence.

Amy squatted down. The hole looked as if it had been dug recently. And there was a tuft of red fur caught on the base of the chicken wire. 'Fox!' she whispered. 'I knew it!'

'Looks like you were right, Amy,' Boo said. 'He's tricked them into leaving the pens.'

'Let's see if we can find any clues,' Ruth suggested. 'We need to be sure they've gone to the college.'

The three chickens burrowed through the hole and scuttled towards the deserted coops. It was the first time they had actually visited the chicken pens. Amy thought what a lovely place it was. Or it would have been if it were full of chickens. There were about a dozen coops, all painted bright colours, tucked away amongst the trees. The little hen houses were made of wood with sloping red roofs, built up on stilts of brick. To get in you had to hop up a ramp and through a door. Amy thought they looked very comfortable. There was even a roosting box built out to one side where you could go if you felt broody.

One of the coops had lots of tiny muddy footprints leading up and down the ramp.

'This must be the school,' Amy said. She scuttled up the ramp to investigate. There was a piece of paper pinned to the door. Amy read it carefully.

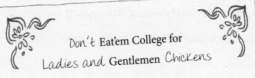

Don't Eat'em College for
Ladies and Gentlemen Chickens

Invites you to
an Open Evening and Fair
Tonight at 6.00 pm

Barbecue!

Semolina!

Games and Prizes!

Bring the family and all your friends!

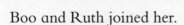

Don't Eat'em College for
Ladies and Gentlemen Chickens

The Deep Dark Woods
Dudley Estate,
Berkshire

Boo and Ruth joined her.

'It's just as we feared,' Amy said. 'The chicks and their parents have gone to Eat'em College for the barbecue, not realising it's them on the menu!'

'We need to hurry,' Ruth said. 'We've got to stop Fox.'

'How though?' Boo asked as they descended the ramp. 'I'm not being a scaredy-hen, but we don't have a plan.'

Amy and Boo both looked at Ruth.

'Hmm . . .' Ruth scratched her head. 'Let's see what's in here. The professor's bound to have thought of something we can use.' She emptied the contents of the Emergency Chicken Pack on the grass. There

were four items. The chickens had never seen any of them before. They regarded them curiously.

'Handy Hawk Kit,' Amy said, selecting a rectangular box. She read from the instructions: 'Takes minutes to assemble. Remote control and batteries included.'

'We can use it to scare the pigeons!' Ruth cried. 'They're terrified of hawks. Here, pass it to me!'

Amy handed it to her. 'Do you know how it works?'

'Easy-peasy,' Ruth said, scrutinising the box.

'What about these?' Next Amy chose two small, labelled plastic bottles. One said 'Essence of Beef', the other, 'Essence of Fish'.

Ruth examined them. 'The professor must have meant these for Kebab Claude and Tiny Tony Tiddles,' she said slowly.

'How?' Amy asked.

'Look.' Ruth held up the bottles so that Amy and Boo could see. 'Each has a dropper on the end so that whoever is using them can lay a trail for Kebab and Claude to follow,' she said.

'I can do that!' Boo offered eagerly. 'I can make it really hard to follow. That would give you enough time to free the chickens.'

'Brilliant,' said Amy. 'That just leaves Fox. What do we do about him?' There was only one item left on the ground. It was a curious funnel-shaped object with a handle. She picked it up. There was some lettering on the side:

VULPES VULPES VOICE CHANGER

'What does that mean?'

'*Vulpes vulpes* is Latin for red fox,' Ruth said thoughtfully. 'I think it means that when you speak through this you sound like one: a red fox, I mean.'

'What good's that going to do?' Boo asked, mystified.

'I don't know,' Ruth admitted. 'Maybe it's to scare him?'

'But Thaddeus E. Fox isn't scared of other foxes,' Boo said. 'Is he?'

Amy shrugged. 'There's only one way to find

out.' She and Ruth stuffed the gadgets back into the Emergency Chicken Pack and the three chickens took off towards the Deep Dark Woods, ready for their mission.

Chapter Fifteen

'There it is!' Amy landed in an old crow's nest at the top of a tall tree. 'Look. Down there.'

Eat'em College for Gentlemen Foxes lay beneath them, a hundred metres in from the edge of the Deep Dark Woods. The chickens peered curiously at the old stone cottage. It was long and low-built with narrow windows. It looked as if it had been designed by humans but then abandoned. The panes of glass were broken. Ivy grew up the walls. The roof was covered in green lichen. In fact, thought Amy, if you didn't know it was there, you might not see it at all. It was almost as if it had been taken over by the Deep Dark Woods and become part of them. Yet there were signs of life. Or death, if you were a chicken, Amy thought. For at one end of the cottage stood a chimney. And from that chimney came a thin trickle of smoke.

'We have to hurry!' Boo said. 'Give me the bottles.'

She made a grab for the Emergency Chicken Pack.

'Wait!' squawked Amy, putting out a wing to stop her. 'Thaddeus E. Fox will be expecting us. He's bound to have someone keeping a lookout.'

'The Pigeon-Poo Gang!' Ruth had donned her super-spec headset. 'They're over there.' She pointed.

Amy peered down. Hidden amongst the tangled ivy were the three pigeons.

'Pass me the Handy Hawk Kit,' Ruth ordered.

Amy handed the box to Ruth.

'Hold these.' Ruth placed two cylindrical-shaped objects in Amy's wings and got to work with the screwdriver.

'What are they?' Amy asked.

'Batteries,' Ruth said. 'Don't drop them. We need them for the remote control.'

Amy held on to them tightly. She watched Ruth in admiration. Honestly, she was glad she didn't have to assemble the hawk. It didn't look very handy at all. She wouldn't have a clue which bit went where. She was glad Ruth was so clever.

'Finished!' Ruth held up the model.

Amy thought it looked really impressive. It had great long wings and a curved beak. From a distance it would be impossible to tell it was made out of cardboard.

'Okay, here goes.' Ruth placed the pretend hawk on the edge of the crow's nest and pushed a button on the remote control. The chickens watched as the pretend hawk flew out of the tree and down towards the roof of the cottage. Once she was satisfied it was within sight of the pigeons, Ruth pressed the 'hover' button. Then she pressed 'circle'.

The hawk's shadow moved in slow, measured loops above the dilapidated roof, as if it were looking for prey.

Amy heard a petrified cooing. The Pigeon-Poo Gang flew up in a confused flutter of grey and purple. 'It's working!' Her voice trembled with excitement. 'They're leaving!'

The terrified pigeons disappeared into the woods.

'Great work, Ruth!' Amy said.

'Okay,' Boo took a deep breath. 'Now it's my turn.'

Amy took the two small plastic bottles out of the Emergency Chicken Pack. She held them out to Boo.

'You don't need to take the bottles,' Ruth said quickly. 'Here.' Gently she squeezed the rubber stopper on the top of each one; then let go of them gradually. Amy watched, fascinated as the liquid inside the bottles sucked up the tube. It was like magic!

'Simple difference in pressure,' Ruth explained. 'When you squeeze the stopper it pushes the air out. When you put it in the bottle the liquid is drawn up inside.'

'Oh,' said Amy. She wished she'd paid more attention in science.

Ruth removed the droppers and gave them to Boo.

Boo tucked them under her wings. She smiled. 'Don't worry, Amy,' she said. 'I'll be fine this time.'

Amy gave her a quick hug. After all, Professor Rooster wasn't there to see! And anyway, Boo deserved it for being so brave. 'Good luck,' she whispered.

Boo launched herself from the crow's nest. She fluttered elegantly down from the tree, her feathered boots brushing the branches, and landed lightly on the ground close to the door of the cottage. Amy watched, her heart in her mouth. *Please let none of the foxes come out now*, she prayed.

In the blink of an eye Boo squeezed a drop from each bottle on the doorstep and somersaulted under a bramble bush. From there she vaulted on to a fallen branch and squeezed two more drops of essence underneath it amongst some mouldy leaves.

Then she raced along the branch, grabbed a twig and did a complicated dismount into a rabbit hole. Seconds later she emerged from the rabbit hole and somersaulted this way and that, deeper and deeper into the Deep Dark Woods until after a while she disappeared from Amy's view.

'Any minute now . . .' Ruth predicted.

Suddenly the door of the stone cottage was thrown open.

Tiny Tony Tiddles came out, closely followed by Kebab Claude.

Tiny Tony lifted his head. 'Fish!' he said. 'I knew I could smell something even more delicious than chicken.'

Kebab Claude's chops drooled. 'Beef!' he sighed. 'I want it.'

The two villains dropped their noses to the ground and started to follow the false trail that Boo had laid. Very soon they disappeared as well.

'Do you think she'll be all right?' Ruth asked anxiously.

Amy had no doubt. 'Of course she will,' she said.

'She's a chicken on a mission. Like us.' Amy glanced at the chimney. The trickle of smoke was getting thicker. 'It's up to us to deal with Thaddeus and his pals,' she said.

'But what are we going to do?' Ruth squawked.

'I have absolutely no idea,' Amy said. 'But I've got a feeling this may come in handy.' Clutching the voice changer in one wing, Amy flew towards the cottage. She settled on a convenient branch and looked in through the broken window.

Chapter Seventeen

'Phwa ha ha ha ha!' Thaddeus E. Fox was enjoying himself. What could be better than this? He was in the Great Dining Hall at Eat'em College for Gentlemen Foxes, lording it over some of his favourite old school pals. Above him, dangling from the rafters by their feet, were all the chicks from Dudley Coop Academy and their parents and teachers who had turned up for the Don't Eat'em College for Ladies and Gentlemen Chickens Open Evening and Fair. In one corner was a huge bowl of lumpy custard to serve with the chickens once they were cooked. And in the other was a packet of semolina as a reward for the Pigeon-Poo Gang once they had made sure the coast was clear of Rooster and his annoying chicken squad.

So far, as Thaddeus E. Fox had expected, everything was going according to his brilliantly conceived plan.

'How's the barbecue coming along, Claude?' he shouted. Kebab Claude had set up his grill in the fireplace.

There was no answer. Thaddeus E. Fox looked around the hall. He couldn't see Claude anywhere. Nor could he see Tiny Tony Tiddles. They must have gone to collect more wood for the fire.

Thaddeus E. Fox turned his attention back to his friends. He surveyed the room with pride. It was a good turnout this year, thanks to his promise of freshly grilled chicken. Crowds of foxes sat on benches either side of long trestle tables, talking excitedly. They were all dressed in the traditional Eat'em uniform – top hat, tails and silk waistcoats. Thaddeus E. Fox sighed with pleasure. It was a sight that made him feel good to be alive, especially as it wouldn't be long before the chickens weren't.

'Thaddeus, old man!' A handsome fox with thick fur and a well brushed tail clapped him on the shoulder with his paw.

'Snooty Bush!' Thaddeus cried. 'I haven't seen you for years!'

Snooty Bush shrugged. 'I've moved to the town,' he said. 'It's so much cooler than living round here. We go on bin raids every night. And sleep in until lunchtime. And there are loads of hen parties. Whereabouts are you these days?'

'Here,' Thaddeus E. Fox said shortly.

'What, still in the Deep Dark Woods?' Snooty Bush raised an eyebrow.

'Yes.'

You're not living in that old burrow your dad dug, are you?'

'Yes.'

Snooty Bush gave him a snooty look. 'You should get out more,' he said.

Thaddeus E. Fox didn't reply. He'd forgotten what a know-it-all show-off Snooty Bush was. To his annoyance Snooty Bush sat down beside him.

'You know what?' Snooty Bush glanced around the walls of the Great Dining Hall. 'I reckon I'll be so famous one day I'll get my portrait up there.'

The wood-panelled walls were covered with pictures of famous old Eat'emians. There was

Sherlock Fox, the famous detective; Count Dracu-Fox, the bloodsucker; and General Fox Kitchen, who won the famous Battle of the Deep Dark Woods against the badgers in 1918.

'Good for you,' Thaddeus E. Fox said sourly. He wished he had something to boast about. His eye fell on a huge painting at the end of the hall, which rested on the mantelpiece above the fire. The painting was of the two hundredth headmaster of Eat'em College, Bertram Fox-William Tail-Spanker, deceased. Seeing the face of the horrible headmaster gave Thaddeus E. Fox an idea.

'Hey, Snooty, remember old Tail-Spanker?' Thaddeus E. Fox said. 'He once whacked me ten times with a recorder for being rude in music.'

'So what?' Snooty Bush guffawed. 'He once whacked me twenty times with a ruler for snoring in science,' he yawned.

'Oh yeah?' Thaddeus E. Fox's eyes narrowed. 'Well, he once whacked me fifty times with a pencil for giggling in Greek.'

Snooty Bush picked up a beetle from the floor and

flicked it expertly at the portrait. It whizzed across the room and smacked the portrait on the nose. 'That's nothing,' he sneered. 'He once whacked me a hundred times with a exercise book for farting in French.'

The two foxes started to argue furiously, each one trying to outdo the other with their stories of the terrible Tail-Spanker.

Amy and Boo sat on the branch watching closely.

'That snooty fox is really winding Thaddeus up,' Ruth observed.

'But he's not actually *afraid* of him,' Amy said. 'He just doesn't like him.'

'He seems quite afraid of Bertram Fox-William Tail-Spanker, though,' Ruth said.

'That's true,' Amy agreed. 'But he's dead . . .' Even as she said it, Amy knew that she had just had a tiny flash of chicken genius.

The two chickens looked at one another.

'That's it!' Ruth said. 'Tail-Spanker!'

'The voice changer!' Amy said. 'I can pretend to be his ghost!'

'Am I missing something?' Just then Boo rejoined the group.

'Thaddeus E. Fox is scared of his old headmaster,' Amy explained gleefully. 'So is the snooty fox he's arguing with. They probably all are. If they think Bertram Fox-William Tail-Spanker has come back to haunt them then they might run away!'

'Where are Kebab Claude and Tiny Tony Tiddles?' Ruth asked.

'Being chased by a badger on the other side of the Deep Dark Woods,' Boo said. 'I put some of the essence down its sett. It didn't look too pleased when Tiddles and Claude dropped in.'

'Well done, Boo,' Amy said. She turned her attention back to the foxes. 'I've got to get behind that picture.'

Ruth pointed upwards. 'Go along the rafters,' she said. 'They won't see you if you're with all the other chickens.'

'Okay,' Amy said. 'Wish me luck!' She ducked

through the window, being careful not to cut her toes on the broken glass, and pushed the 'up' button on the flight booster.

ZOOM! She shot up to the wooden beams where the chickens were being held captive and landed amongst the chicks. They started cheeping frantically.

'Shhhh,' she told them sternly. She didn't want the Month 4s ruining everything again. 'I'll free you in a minute. Now pipe down before the foxes hear you.'

The chicks were silent.

Amy crept along the rafter towards the painting.

Beneath her she could hear the two foxes still arguing about their old headmaster.

'Call that a whacking?' Thaddeus E. Fox shouted. 'He once whacked me five hundred times with a rubber for laughing in Latin.'

Amy reached the painting. It was propped up on the mantelpiece. She noticed there was a narrow gap behind it at the bottom where it stood out from the wall. Amy eyed the gap carefully. If she pulled her

tummy in she might just be able to squeeze behind the picture with the voice changer.

Checking none of the foxes were watching, she took off her flight-booster engine, dropped down from the rafter on to the mantelpiece and wriggled into the gap. Amy breathed a sigh of relief. The foxes hadn't seen her.

'Big deal!' Snooty Bush yelled back. 'He once whacked me a thousand times with a whistle for spitting in sport.'

Amy made a tiny hole in the canvas with her toe so that she could see the foxes. They were all engrossed in the argument. They seemed to have forgotten about the banquet, for the moment at least. This was her chance. She gave a little cough and raised the voice changer to her mouth.

'SHUT UP!' Amy shouted. She was surprised to hear a terrible voice ring round the cottage. Then she realised it was hers! At least it was *her* speaking but the voice changer had made her sound like a very cross and cranky old fox: Bertram Fox-William Tail-Spanker, to be precise.

Amy peeped through the hole in the canvas. The effect on the foxes was electrifying. They were all staring at the painting, pointing and barking excitedly. She gave another little cough then tried again.

'I SAID SHUT UP,' her voice boomed. 'OR I'LL WHACK YOU ALL A MILLION TIMES WITH MY . . . ER . . . TOENAIL CLIPPERS!'

She put her eye to the hole. She was pleased to see that both Thaddeus E. Fox and his snooty pal looked petrified.

'It's old Tail-Spanker!' Snooty Bush gasped.

'But he's dead!' Thaddeus E. Fox blinked.

Amy giggled. She was beginning to enjoy herself. It was fun being Tail-Spanker. She spoke into the voice changer.

'I MIGHT BE DEAD BUT I CAN STILL GIVE YOU A GOOD WHACKING!' she shouted. 'WE TAIL-SPANKERS DON'T STOP JUST BECAUSE WE'VE KICKED THE BUCKET.'

She took another look through the hole. To her joy the foxes were getting ready to leave.

'I'm going back to the city!' Snooty Bush picked up his top hat and dashed out of the door. 'It's safer.'

'Wait for us!' The rest of the Gentlemen foxes chased after him.

Very soon only Thaddeus E. Fox remained. 'But . . .' he said uncertainly, gazing hard at the picture.

Amy frowned. He was proving hard to dislodge. She raised the voice changer.

'BUTT, BUM, BACKSIDE, BOTTOM,' she yelled. 'I DON'T CARE WHAT YOU CALL IT, FOX. IT'S ALL THE SAME TO ME. I'LL WHACK IT! ESPECIALLY IF IT BELONGS TO YOU, YOUNG THADDEUS.'

'I . . .' Thaddeus E. Fox began. He was braver than the other foxes.

'HOW DARE YOU SPEAK BACK TO ME??!!' Amy thundered. 'NOW BEAK IT, OR I'LL COME OUT THERE AND WHACK YOU.' She tapped her beak on the voice changer mouthpiece. KNOCK. KNOCK. KNOCK. KNOCK. The sound was magnified a zillion times. It sounded as though a

huge cross fox was banging at the picture, trying to get out. The noise echoed around the empty room. Up above in the rafters, the captive chickens squawked in terror.

The cacophony of noise was too much for Thaddeus E. Fox. 'Don't worry, I'm going,' he yelped.

Amy put her eye to the hole. She grinned at what she saw. She'd done it! Thaddeus E. Fox was spooked. He rammed his top hat on his head, grabbed his cane and fled.

Chapter Eighteen

'You can come out now, Amy.'

It was Ruth's voice. It was coming from the rafters. She and Boo must be up there untying the chickens, Amy realised.

'Okay,' Amy tried to wriggle her way out. To her dismay she found she couldn't. She was sandwiched behind the portrait of Bertram Fox–William Tail-Spanker.

'They've all gone, Amy!' Boo's voice floated down. 'Now hurry up and give us a hand to free the chickens before the foxes discover it's a trick.'

'I can't!' Amy said. 'I'm stuck.'

'Breathe in,' Boo suggested.

Amy breathed in. She wriggled some more. But the more she wriggled the faster she became stuck.

'Rip the painting,' Ruth advised.

Amy raised her toe to the little hole and tried to make it bigger. But the canvas was tough. Try as she

might she couldn't get anywhere. And it was hard work balancing on one leg in such a small space. She fell over.

'Help me move the painting, can't you?' Amy tried to push against the frame but the picture wouldn't budge.

'In a minute,' Boo said. 'We're just freeing the chickens.'

Amy could hear the sound of cheeping and squawking as the prisoners were released.

Amy heaved against the painting again.

'Don't worry,' Ruth was saying, 'we'll soon have you down.'

'Help!' Amy said. She was beginning to feel quite scared.

'There, that's the lot,' Ruth said. 'Go and help Amy, Boo.'

To Amy's relief Boo's strong wing wrapped itself around the picture frame. 'Push,' Boo said. Amy strained against the painting. 'It's no good!' she panted. 'It won't budge.'

'Get into groups,' Ruth took charge of the freed

chickens. 'Stick with the other chickens from your coops.'

Even though she was scared, Amy felt proud of Ruth. Ruth sounded just like a real teacher: not a horrible one like Bertram Fox-William Tail-Spanker, but a nice, kind, sensible one who knew what to do. Amy peeped through the hole. The chickens were organising themselves as Ruth had asked. Even the chicks were doing what Ruth told them.

'One grown-up in charge of each group,' Ruth said calmly.

She hopped over to the painting. 'What's happening?' Ruth's voice subsided to a hiss. 'Where's Amy?'

'She can't get out,' Boo replied in a whisper. 'You go with the chickens back to the pens, Ruth. I'll stay and help her.'

'No!' Amy squawked from behind the portrait. 'Go with Ruth.'

'I'm staying,' Boo said in a firm tone.

'All right,' Ruth agreed. 'But you'd better hurry.

It won't be long before Fox and his gang work out it was a trick. Good luck, you two.'

Ruth led the chickens at a brisk trot out of the door and into the Deep Dark Woods in the direction of the chicken pens.

'Don't worry, Amy,' Boo said. 'We'll soon get you out of there. I'll see if I can find a sharp stick or something to slash the painting.' She disappeared too.

Amy was left alone. She waited.

After a little while there was a scuffling sound at the entrance to the Great Dining Hall.

Amy listened hard. It didn't sound like Boo. She looked through the hole in the canvas. Amy gulped. Her knees started to knock. It was Thaddeus E. Fox! He was back. And that meant he suspected he had been tricked. And it wasn't just Fox either. He was closely followed by two other members of the MOST WANTED Club: Kebab Claude and Tiny Tony Tiddles.

Amy raised the voice changer with a trembling wing. 'WHO DARES DISTURB THE GHOST

Bertram Fox-William Tail-Spanker.

OF THE GREAT BERTRAM FOX–WILLIAM
TAIL-SPANKER?' she squeaked. Even to her the
voice didn't sound very convincing this time.

'Who was that?' Kebab Claude asked nervously.

'That's what I'm intending to find out,' Thaddeus
E. Fox replied.

'The chickens have escaped,' Tiny Tony Tiddles'

voice was full of disgust. 'How did you let that happen?'

'For the same reason you disappeared out of the door and ended up having a fight with a badger,' Thaddeus E. Fox snapped back. 'I was tricked. I think our friend Professor Rooster has been busy,' he growled, 'with his little chicken squad.'

Behind the painting Amy's breath came in short rasps. There wasn't any point in pretending to be the ghost of Bertram Fox–William Tail-Spanker any more. She was doomed!

'You mean . . .' Kebab Claude began.

'I mean they scared off the pigeons somehow and laid a false trail to get you and Tony out of the way,' Thaddeus E. Fox said. 'And then one of them got in here and used some kind of machine to make it sound like the picture was talking so that all the foxes left. Am I right?'

With a shock, Amy realised his voice was directed straight at the picture. She felt like crying. He was talking to *her*! She hoped Boo was safe.

'The reason I know all of this,' Thaddeus E.

Fox continued conversationally, 'is because when I got back to the burrow it occurred to me that the headmaster of Eat'em College for Gentlemen Foxes would never use the word butt. Or bum for that matter. And he certainly wouldn't say "beak it".' He was still addressing the painting.

Amy could have kicked herself for being so stupid. She should have used posher words! She knew she should have paid more attention in English.

'Great. So now *you've* been duped by a bunch of birds,' Tiny Tony Tiddles said sourly, 'like the rest of us. We might as well pack it in and go home. There ain't gonna be no banquet. The chickens have all gone.'

'Maybe not *all* of them,' Thaddeus E. Fox said in a steely voice. 'Let's see. Kebab, give me some help.'

To Amy's horror the picture started to rock. A foxy paw appeared around one edge of the frame. A doggy one appeared around the other.

'Lift!'

The painting began to rise. Amy dug her toes into the groove between the frame and the canvas.

She had to take them by surprise if she was to have any chance of escaping.

'Heave!' The picture rose further into the air with Amy still riding on the back of it.

'Put it down.'

The portrait was lowered to the floor.

'Now tip it forwards. Claude, see what's behind it.'

Amy braced herself. She raised the voice changer in both wings to use as a weapon.

Kebab's head appeared around the edge of the canvas.

BANG! Amy forced the voice changer over his nose as hard as she could. 'Have a new muzzle!' she squawked. 'Courtesy of Professor Rooster.' She plunged off the painting and raced towards the door.

Kebab Claude staggered around the hall, his nose in the funnel. ''ELP!' he snorted. 'I can't breathe!'

'Not so fast, sister.' Tony Tiddles appeared in front of Amy. He licked his lips.

'Up here, hoodlum!' Amy glanced up. It was

Boo! She was balancing on the rafters. Amy didn't think she'd ever been so pleased to see anyone in her life before.

'You get that one, Tony,' Thaddeus E. Fox snarled. 'And I'll eat the little fat juicy one.'

Tiny Tony Tiddles scrambled up the wall towards the rafters.

Seeing Boo had given Amy courage. 'Come on then, Fox.' She started running round in circles, looking for a patch of dirt. It was the only thing left to try: the feather dusty. She wouldn't go down without a fight: especially not to Thaddeus E. Fox. 'Prepare to get your butt kicked.'

'Ooh, I'm scared,' he said.

'You should be.' Amy's circling had revealed something even better than a patch of dirt. In the corner beside Kebab Claude's grill was an enormous bowl of lumpy custard. She headed towards it and landed in it with a flump. The custard oozed between her fluffy tummy feathers.

'Yum,' Thaddeus E. Fox said. 'Chicken with lumpy custard. My favourite Eat'em dish.' He advanced

towards Amy, his tongue lolling from between his teeth.

'You okay, Boo?' Amy glanced up again.

'Never better.' Boo was doing somersaults and backflips along the beam.

Tiny Tony Tiddles was trying his hardest to catch her but Amy could tell from the dazed look in the cat's eyes that he was getting dizzy trying to follow Boo's gymnastic moves.

Amy had a final wriggle in the custard, then leaped out of the bowl and started to run as fast as she could for takeoff, flapping her wings furiously. 'Phew!' Amy puffed. She'd forgotten how hard it was to get off the ground without the flight booster, especially with a tummy dripping with custard.

BANG!

Thaddeus E. Fox tried to hit her with his cane.

Amy dodged him. *Come on*, she told herself. *Come on.*

'You can do it, Amy!' Boo urged. 'I know you can.'

Amy made one final effort and launched herself into the air. Slowly she gained height.

Thaddeus E. Fox thrashed at her. 'Come here!' he snarled.

CRASH!

Amy looked down. Tiny Tony Tiddles had fallen off the beam. 'Your plan sucks, Fox!' he said. He limped out of the cottage and disappeared.

'Great work, Boo!' Amy cried. She did one more loop of the room and locked on to her target. With one final whoop, Amy launched herself at Thaddeus E. Fox.

BASH! Her momentum knocked him to the ground. Thaddeus E. Fox lay on his back, his legs in the air, with a small custard-covered chicken wrapped around his whiskers.

'Get off!' he spluttered. The lumpy custard was in his eyes. It was in his mouth. It was in his whiskers. It was clogging up his fur.

'Shan't!' Amy rubbed her tummy in his face.

'What move do you call that?' Boo shouted from the rafters.

'The feather *custy*!' Amy shrieked.

'You're smothering me!' Thaddeus E. Fox coughed. The custard was going up his nose! He couldn't breathe. With a howl of anger he pushed Amy off.

Amy felt herself being catapulted through the air. She landed in a heap under one of the trestle tables.

Thaddeus E. Fox padded towards her.

Amy tried to move but she couldn't. She had used up all her strength. She was finished. 'Get out of here, Boo!' she cried.

'No.' Boo fluttered down beside her. 'We're a team, remember.'

'We certainly are.' Amy heard a third voice behind her. It was Ruth! She'd come back to help them. And, with a thrill of joy, Amy saw that she had brought the mite blaster with her. 'Get out of the way, you two!' Ruth shouted.

Amy felt Boo's strong wings grab her by the legs and pull her across the floor.

'Get ready to itch, Fox!' Ruth yelled.

 171

BOOMPH! Ruth pulled the trigger of the mite blaster.

The cloud of insects hit Thaddeus E. Fox in the face.

To Amy's horror, he shook them off. 'No mite would dare attack me!' he cried. 'Besides,' he threw a sideways glance at Amy, 'they can't get through the custard!' Thaddeus E. Fox stalked towards Ruth.

'That's what you think, Fox!' *BOOMPH!* Ruth hit him again. *BOOMPH!* And again. *BOOMPH! BOOMPH!*

Thaddeus E. Fox stopped. 'Ouch!' He put a paw to his whiskers and started to scratch. 'Ooohhh!' He put a paw to his ears. 'Aarrggghhh!' Soon he was scratching frantically all around his chin. Great big lumpy bite marks appeared on his face.

'It actually seems as if the custard is making the mites bite harder,' Ruth observed with interest. *BOOMPH!* 'Have another blast.'

With one last backward glance at the chickens, Thaddeus E. Fox staggered out of the door. 'I'll get you for this!' he roared. 'And Rooster. Just you wait

and see.' Then he disappeared into the Deep Dark Woods.

Kebab Claude pulled the voice changer off his nose and cantered after him.

After they'd gone, the three chickens lay on their backs with their legs in the air, exhausted. They held wings.

'That was the most terrifying thing I've ever done in my life,' Boo said.

'Me too,' Ruth agreed.

'Me too, but you've got to admit it was kind of fun,' Amy said.

The three chickens stared up at the roof of the cottage. There was silence for a few minutes.

'You know,' Boo said. 'I'm beginning to think I *am* cut out for this.'

'Me too,' Ruth agreed.

'That makes three of us,' Amy said. Her cheeks glowed. 'I can't wait for our next mission.' She thought how happy she was to have made such good friends. And what a brilliant team they made together. Courage, intelligence and perseverance:

 174

Shigong Egg was right – those *were* the ingredients you needed to succeed. And Professor Rooster would be pleased: they'd sent the MOST WANTED villains packing without any help from James Pond. Amy sighed happily. Life was good. 'Chicken mission accomplished,' she said.

Epilogue

Shigong Egg was in the middle of a headstand when Menial came in with the newspaper. He'd been like that for three days already and had another four to go.

'Place it on my feet, Menial,' Shigong Egg commanded. 'With an apple if you would.'

'A red one, Master?' Menial asked.

'Red is the colour of lips, chips and cherry pips,' Shigong Egg breathed.

'Surely not chips, Master?' Menial said.

'Of course, chips, Menial, if they have ketchup on,' Shigong Egg said crossly. 'Do you doubt my wisdom?'

'No, Master. Only a fool would do that.' Menial placed the newspaper and a red apple on Shigong Egg's toes and shuffled out.

Shigong Egg brought his knees to his chest. Slowly he straightened one leg so that the foot with the

apple hovered in front of his mouth. He stretched his toes and took a bite. Then he straightened the other leg so that the newspaper was in front of his eyes.

ROOSTER AND HIS TEAM DEFEAT FOX AND THE MOST WANTED CLUB

'Ah!' Shigong Egg took another bite of his apple. 'It is as I said it would be. Through difference comes unity.'

With a contented sigh Shigong Egg turned to the back page and started working out the crossword.

Don't miss . . .

Out Now!

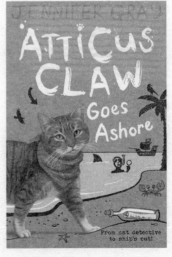

Join Agent Cluckbucket and her friends for more adventures in the next book. Coming in February 2015. Keep a beady eye out for it!

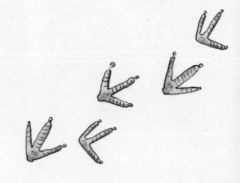